Taking Our Time

First published 1979 by Pluto Press Limited
Unit 10 Spencer Court, 7 Chalcot Road, London NW1 8LH

Pluto Press gratefully acknowledges financial
assistance from the Calouste Gulbenkian Foundation,
Lisbon, with the publication of this series

ISBN 0 86104 210 7

Designed by Tom Sullivan
Cover designed by Kate Hepburn
Cover picture: 'Plug Rioters at Salterhebble' from the
    Illustrated London News, August 1842

Printed in Great Britain by Latimer Trend & Company Ltd Plymouth

Red Ladder

Taking Our Time

Pluto  Plays

'From the loom, the factory and the mine, Good Lord deliver us.'

Chartist Prayer

'Your complaint is *machinery*, and the remedy is the Charter.'

Fergus O'Connor

A NOTE ON THE PRODUCTION

Taking Our Time was written and produced for West Yorkshire working-class audiences who are not, on the whole, theatregoers. The reality of reaching these audiences is a central part of Red Ladder's work. Theatres and arts centres do not usually attract potential working-class audiences: the cultural aura of 'the theatre' is often alien and the plays put on in many theatres bear little relevance to the experience of working-class life. Getting to and from a theatre can also be a problem: the journey from the Pennine valleys of West Yorkshire to the Leeds Playhouse (the nearest rep) is costly and difficult, especially on public transport. So Red Ladder is a touring company: we take our shows to our audiences.

Taking Our Time was performed in forty different venues in West Yorkshire – working-men's clubs, community centres, schools and colleges. It reached 10,000 people in the county between January and June 1978. It was also toured in London, South Yorkshire, South Lancashire, the Midlands and Scotland.

The organisation of these tours was central to the show's success. Many of the venues had never put on a piece of theatre before. Opening them up for our show was challenging and difficult. It often required months of painstaking negotiation with club committees, worried for their bar profits, doubtful about getting an audience, and wary of the political sounding nature of the play. And even when the venue had been won the task of getting the audience to it could not be left to a few randomly placed posters and a scattering of handouts. Trade Unions, Community Associations and schools needed to be convinced to sponsor and organise their members and pupils to go to the performance. Publicity had to be sufficiently thorough to draw any potentially interested people in the county as a whole.

A touring theatre needs to travel as lightly as possible. Complicated sets are not desirable. We performed this play on a bare stage of four stepped levels. Props were minimal but as authentic as we could make or find: stools, pans, the rifle, etc. We used lights, including a small cyclorama backdrop, to establish the moods of scenes through changes of colour. The music was amplified and so required a certain amount of sound hardware. In the event our 'get-in' and 'get-out' were on the heavy side and took up too much time: setting up took three hours at each venue. The workers' costumes were based on illustrations in *Costumes of Yorkshire* by G. Walker (1814). Some of them wore clogs. Employers' costumes and military uniforms were designed from available plates of the 1840s. The clown's smock was a direct copy from a nineteenth-century fool's smock which we had access to.

INTRODUCTION
by Julian Harber

Factories have not always been with us. Two hundred years ago in Britain, most people in manufacturing industry worked in their own homes or in small workshops. The lives of these people were far from ideal – hours of work were usually long, pay low, life-expectancy short. Most had no political rights. But within the limits of the need to earn enough to survive, many of them did have a substantial amount of control over their work, being able to decide what methods they would use, when to start in the morning, when to finish, when to take time off. In particular, work routines could be varied to accord with changed family circumstances, so the needs of the sick, the young and the elderly could be attended to.

The industrial revolution that began in Britain at the end of the eighteenth century did not initially change all this. For even in the pace-making textile industry, factories were introduced initially only in spinning. The massive increase in the output of woven cloth was not the product of the mills, but of weavers who worked by hand on looms in their own homes. In the early 1790s, the handloom weavers were amongst the best-paid workers in Britain.

The mechanisation of weaving was not long in coming though. Factory production using power looms was introduced first in cotton in the 1810s, then a few years later in wool. The effects on the wages of hundreds of thousands of handloom weavers (and thousands more in attendant trades that were similarly mechanised, such as woolcombing and cropping) were disastrous. 'It is truly lamentable to behold so many thousands of men who formerly earned twenty to thirty shillings per week, now compelled to live upon five shillings, four shillings or even less,' wrote the great radical journalist William Cobbett of the Halifax district in 1832.

The coming of the factories, however, did not just catastrophically reduce the handloom weavers' income, but undermined their very way of life. For though proclaimed as progress by the masters and government, the factories meant not just regulation and regimentation – clocking in and out, the discipline of the foreman and the factory hooter – but the reduction of work to simple drudgery and the breakdown of traditional domestic arrangements. 'They take a man now for his muscular appearance not for his talent – machines have become so simple that attending them is commonplace labour,' complained an Ashton textile worker in 1840. 'The ruthless hand of the oppressor has dragged our wives and little ones into the factory or loathesome mine . . . whilst the father and the husband is an unwilling idler and a pauper, living upon the blood and vitals of those he loves,' complained another, William Dixon, a weaver in nearby Middleton, a short time later.

The new factories were also dirty and frequently very dangerous places. To work in them often necessitated a move from the hamlets of the Pennine uplands into the new towns cramped in valley bottoms, choked with smoke and grime. And the rise of factory production was not continuous – for every few years there were slumps when mill after mill went bankrupt. In the summer of 1842, for instance, some two-thirds of Bolton's cotton workers were without jobs. Measuring the employers' and government's idea of progress against their own experience and finding it wanting, the weavers of Lancashire and Yorkshire turned to political action.

Britain at the time was a highly undemocratic society in which the vast majority of the population was denied the vote. The Chartist movement, founded in London in 1838 (but having its mass base in the manufacturing districts of the North), was the culmination of almost half a century of political agitation by working people. It was centred around six demands – universal male suffrage, annual parliaments, vote by secret ballot, equal electoral districts, payment of MPs and no property qualifications for prospective MPs.

These demands were seen not just as ends in themselves, but as a means whereby working people could control society in their own interests. To the handloom weaver this meant the prospect that the introduction of machinery would be controlled and carried out in a way that would benefit all.

In order to try to get the implementation of the People's Charter, its adherents tried a variety of methods – monster meetings, petitions, strikes and armed insurrection.

The Great Strike of 1842 originated in Ashton-under-Lyne soon after a petition bearing more than three million signatures in favour of the Charter had been rejected by the House of Commons. Traditionally, most historians have treated the strike as economic – a spontaneous outburst against wage-cuts, unemployment and hunger – which somehow the Chartists managed to latch on to after the event. But recent research has confirmed the situation was rather more complex than that.

What is certainly true is that the strike was not called by the National Chartist Association and was only endorsed by their executive after the event. But the idea of a general political strike – or national holiday – had been in the air in radical circles in the months following the rejection of the Charter by Parliament, it being strongly advocated by one faction of the Chartist movement around the fiery McDouall – a man with a very strong following in the North. And right from the start the local leadership of the strike in locality after locality was not just Chartist, but often consisted of people with a decade or more of involvement in radical politics behind them. Nor was it a matter either of a political leadership leading a non-political rank and file. In Oldham, for instance, after a keen debate, a mass movement of strikers voted by an overwhelming show of hands that the strike was not about 'a fair day's work for a fair day's pay', but about staying out until the Charter became the law of the land. This is not to suggest that the strike was consciously planned by Chartists – though this cannot be entirely ruled out. But it is possible that there was some agreement amongst the followers of McDouall to 'seize the time' should the opportunity present itself.

In any event the strike moved like a bushfire through Lancashire, quickly crossed the Pennines into Yorkshire and spread as far as the South Midlands, South Wales and up into Scotland, drawing in workers not just from textiles, but from many other trades as well.

In area after area – whether in the huge city of Manchester, the large towns of Rochdale, Stockport and Huddersfield or the industrial villages of the upper Calder Valley such as Luddenden and Ripponden – the pattern was the same; crowds would march to the factories, the sluice gates of the dams supplying them with water would be opened, the plugs of the boilers removed and the workers pulled out on strike. The crowd (now including many of those just pulled out) would then march on the next centre of population where the process would be repeated.

'The sight was just one of those which it is impossible to forget,' recalled the Spen Valley historian Frank Peel some forty years later, of the march from Horton to Bradford. 'They came pouring down the wide road in thousands taking up its whole breadth – a gaunt famished-looking desperate multitude, armed with huge bludgeons, flails, pitch-forks and pikes, many without coats and hats and hundreds upon hundreds in rags and tatters. Many of the older men looked footsore and weary, but the great bulk were men in the prime of life, full of wild excitement. As they marched they thundered out to a grand old tune, a stirring melody.'

In Yorkshire the central drama took place in Halifax, which despite determined action by the authorities the crowds entered from both Bradford and Todmorden. On the night of fourteenth and fifteenth August, at least ten thousand camped out above the town on Skircoat Moor. The crowds were not dispersed until an abortive attack on Akroyd's mill and house at Haley Hill two days later.

The 'Plug Plot' movement (as it subsequently became known) was a failure, though had other parts of the country, notably London, moved together with Lancashire and Yorkshire, the result might have been very different. And though it survived another decade after 1842, the Chartist movement went down in defeat. But the factory owners of the North were certainly very shaken by the events of 1842. In many instances they clearly made efforts subsequently to placate (and control) the working class. Akroyd himself for instance built two 'model villages' – Akroydon and Copley – for his employees to live in.

The problems of the handloom weavers are, it might seem, remote from us in time. But some of the questions they posed, and attempted to answer, in the 1840s – the purpose and nature of economic growth and the human consequences of technological change – still haunt us today.

Julian Harber
Halifax
August 1978

Taking Our Time

The decision to make a history play based on past events in the West Riding was taken with the intention of reconnecting our audiences with that past. But the period we chose needed to have specific resonances with the contemporary experience of our audiences if it was to be of more than passing interest to them. So we chose the 1840s with the aim of drawing from that time some useful parallels for today and some challenging ideas for tomorrow. *Taking Our Time* is set in Halifax and one of its outlying villages in the summer of 1842.

This was a time of transition: a period of great economic and political upheaval. It marked the end of the first stage of the industrial revolution and saw the emergence of a new class. Millions of people had been swept off the land by the enclosures of the late eighteenth and early nineteenth centuries; millions of families of artisans and craftspeople had been put out of work by the mechanisation of their trades and these people were sucked into the new factory system as wage workers. They became the new Working Class. Putting the year 1842 in the spotlight, we hoped to identify what 'qualities of life' were lost in this transition with a view to suggesting what parts of it might be regained in a socialist future.

There were two pitfalls. The first was the danger of painting too golden a picture of life prior to the industrial revolution. For while the actual change from old to new created terrible conditions for most working people, the retrospective picture is one of improved standards of living. Life before was harsh, so we had to think carefully before presenting aspects of it as better. The second danger was that of denying the progressive technological sides of industrial capitalism by laying an undue emphasis on the anti-machine consciousness of the characters we created. In our final product we felt we had only partially avoided these traps.

On the whole, handloom weavers owned their own looms. Like woolcombers, cobblers and other artisans they owned their own means of production. This didn't mean they did not have to work hard. When prices were low and markets were bad the work was gruelling and often there was no work at all. But it did mean that their time, in a certain sense, was their own: they could work when they wanted and needed to rather than be dictated to by an employer's clock. When times were good this freedom to work when and as they pleased resulted in a positive control over their own lives. The tradition of St Monday was based on this freedom and was common all over Europe. It was the long weekend when self-employed craftspeople could decide for themselves to take Monday off, and sometimes even Tuesday. With the industrial revolution the means of production were taken out of their hands and became the property of the employer. St Monday consequently disappeared and with it a crucial aspect of workers' control. We wanted to suggest in the play that with a shorter working week St Monday might be regained today.

Linked with the theme of time is that of the destruction of a popular culture. Before the industrial revolution working people's cultural life was largely self-created. From the more brutal bloodsports of bull baiting, bear baiting and cock fighting, to football matches involving whole towns in the game, to dancing, music, ale-making, fairs, in fact in the whole fabric of cultural life, the keynote was participation and self-provision. This is a far cry from today when the more tangible forms of cultural activity – sport, music, films, etc. – are experienced by most people vicariously as marketed commodities. And when even active pastimes – fishing, gardening, camping – are inextricably tied up with big business.

We wanted to show when and why the destruction of this popular culture took place; and we used the conflict between the preacher and the clown to describe it. Tom Tinker is based on travelling tinkers of the time who used clowning to ply their trade; a clown called Old Crafty is recorded as being active at fairs around Slaithwaite in those years. Tom embodies the dying end of a popular culture. For the orthodox methodist preacher he is the devil incarnate. Because Tom encourages fun and enjoyment: a fullness of life that is anathema to both the stoic requirements of methodism and the disciplinary requirements of Akroyd's new mills. Tom is not the only cultural target of church and employer. The woolcombers – who had a strong republican tradition – are recorded among their many cultural activities as having made their own plays and gone to the length of hiring halls to perform them in. Our play within a play is a speculative reconstruction of one of these 'dramatic presentations' and such goings on came under heavy attack as well. Likewise, singing and dancing, drinking, the activities of the fair were regarded as sinful and idle: ungodly pastimes that showed disrespect for the Lord and were a danger for the disciplinary requirements of the new factory workforce. In pointing to a self-determined culture that was largely destroyed, we hoped to open the possibility in our audiences' minds for an equally self-determined culture of the future.

Experience of the women's movement and sexual politics in our collective led us, in 1974, to make a play specifically about the exploitation and oppression of women – *A Woman's Work Is Never Done*. More recently we have not made sexual politics the single focus of our plays. Instead we have tried to embody a socialist-feminist perspective in the heart of our work. As a result the position of women and the family in *Taking Our Time* was central to our discussion of its themes. But in working this through we had to be careful not to overlay a 1970s' feminist consciousness on the experience of working-class women of the 1840s. The work of Dorothy Thompson on the political and social position of working-class women in the first half of nineteenth-century Britain helped us here.

The 1840s seem to have marked a turning-point for women's experience. In the first half of the century working-class women played an active, often leading, part in the struggles of the time. Newspapers refer to the militant role of women in strikes and demonstrations, and there is evidence of independent women's organisation – Female Chartist Associations – amongst the Chartists. But from the mid-1840s women seem to have retreated from this public political role. Why?

The home of a weaving family in the mid eighteenth century was an integrated productive unit. Housework, spinning, weaving and the tending of a few domestic animals took place under and around the same roof and involved all the family. Although it should be added that men, in these times too, were not renowned for their capacities to do their share of housework. With the industrial revolution, spinning and then weaving left the home for the mechanised mill, while housework, by its very nature, remained behind. Spinning was the first craft to be mechanised. And since it had been the work of women and girls it was they who became the first factory workers. In one sense this was a positive development: it meant that women had gained a relative economic independence, and it was on this independence as wage workers that much of their political prominence in the early nineteenth century was based. But it also created an intolerable burden. For they had to be workers and mothers to their working children in the mills from dawn to dusk; and mothers and wives and house workers in their homes from dusk to dawn. By the 1830s these conditions had led to a factory reform movement pledged to fight for a reduction in working hours for women and children and a raising of the minimum age for childwork in the mills. This movement at first only partially achieved its aims. One result was that women spent marginally more time at home.

Between 1810 and 1830 weaving and then woolcombing were mechanised. By the 1840s most male textile craftsmen had also been displaced from their trades into either unemployment or millwork. With thousands of families, either separated or together, working in mills, the question of 'family life' became a powerful debate amongst the middle classes. Around 1840 there was a spate of pamphlets and books that took up the sorry state of working-class family life. These wrongly indentified mills and factories as dens of vice and promiscuity leading to the bottle, unmarried mothers and unwanted children. The moral fabric of life, they felt, was dangerously threatened. The cause of these evils was attributed to the absence of the mother from the home. So her 'place' was now defined as in that home providing the material and spiritual hearth for her husband and her children.

Coupled with the progressive gains of the factory reform movement, this 'woman's place' ideology led to a partial retreat of working-class women into the home. Women continued to work in factories, but there were fewer mothers among them and they worked shorter hours. The result was a loss in social and political identity: a woman's primary role came to be seen as the wife who fed, clothed and nurtured her work-weary husband, and as the mother who reared and looked after her children – the future workers. But because 'work' was now identified as what took place in factories, in the production of commodities and profits, housework was denied its status as work and became socially invisible. So the basis of the modern nuclear family emerged. In *Taking Our Time* we wanted to show the central role women played in the struggles of the time prior to their enforced 'retreat'. And in Sarah's relationship to William we wanted to infer that this 'retreat' was about to happen.

Lastly, we felt that the struggles of the Chartists had great significance for today. For while the material conditions of life in Britain now are in no way comparable to the dreadful suffering of the 1840s, some of the dynamics of economic life are strikingly similar. In those days the capitalist system was in crisis. The employers, with state support, resorted to harsh wage cutting. Today, it's the same old story: the economy is in crisis, and with state insistence, employers gladly hold back wages in relation to rising prices. In each case an ailing economy is resuscitated at the expense of working people's living standards. But unfortunately, there the similarity ends. For the mass economic and political movement of Chartism was determined in its actions to bring about a people's parliament and a democratically controlled economy, and at times it looked as though they might achieve it. Whereas today the mass commitment to and prospects for such change are not so good.

Red Ladder Theatre

NOTE ON RED LADDER

Red Ladder is a socialist theatre company that has been making and performing plays in the Labour Movement and in working-class industrial communities since 1968. Using Leeds as a base, the company has, for the past few years, been establishing a regional socialist touring theatre company for West and South Yorkshire. Red Ladder works collectively. This does not mean that everybody has a go at everything irrespective of competence. Our division of labour reflects primarily what members are most skilled at. But mobility of job-definition does occur within practicable limits. For example, tour organisers at times become part of the research and writing team and writers at times take on administration. Performers, too, write at times, and some writers perform. The meaning of 'collective' for Red Ladder relates primarily to decision-making: what plays are about, their form, their intended audiences and venues are discussed both outside and inside the company. Final decisions are made by full meetings of company members as are issues of wages, hours, working conditions and all questions of policy.

This form of collective work is in stark contrast to the hierarchies of the establishment theatre in which control rests largely in the hands of management and artistic directors. This power structure is reflected in the form of the credits given to individual theatre workers in programmes and posters. It is all too common to find directors, writers and stars in bold print and at the top of lists; whereas wardrobe, technicians and administrators are relegated to the bottom, in small print, if indeed they appear at all.

In the past, Red Ladder have not credited individuals in programmes and posters because we felt that this would contradict the collective nature of our work. For example, we feel that the tour organising work of an administrator is every bit as important, and in some senses creative, as the imaginative work of writers or performers. We have wanted, and still want, to avoid the public image of a 'pecking order' of apparent influence within the company. Recently, however, some company members felt they wanted individual credit as a form of reference, should the need arise to seek work elsewhere. This was hotly contested, but resulted in a decision to credit as follows:

Costume Design	Barbara Mitchell
	Miriam Dorman
Costume Production	Barbara Mitchell
	Sue Maddock
	Steph Munro
	Jim Roche
Director	Michael Attenborough
Musical Director	Chris Reason
Poster Design	Miriam Dorman
Props	Miriam Dorman
	Gillie Lacey

Set Design/Construction	Simon Best
	Chris Rawlence
Sound Technician/Synthesiser	Simon Best
Lighting Technicians	Kate Housden
	Paul Kleiman
	Tammy Walker
Tour Organisers	Kate Housden
	Paul Kleiman
	Tammy Walker
Financial Administrator	Steph Munro
Authors	Glen Park
	Chris Rawlence
	Steve Trafford
Song Lyrics	Chris Reason
	Steve Trafford
Musical Arrangements	Chris Reason
Historical Advice	Julian Harber
	Arnold Rattenbury
	Dorothy Thompson
	Edward Thompson

Taking Our Time was first produced at East Hunslet Labour Club, Leeds, on 17 January 1978. The cast was as follows:

Mary Greenwood (handloom weaver)	Glen Park
John Greenwood (her husband, handloom weaver)	Gareth Williams
Sarah (mill operative, their daughter)	Elizabeth Mansfield
Jenny (mill operative, their daughter)	Sally Eldridge
Dorothy (maid at Akroyd's, their daughter)	June Parkhurst
Elsie Carter (single parent and millworker)	June Parkhurst
Annie Edwards (handloom weaver)	Sally Eldridge
Peter (woolcomber)	Nick Jensen
Tom Tinker (tinker and travelling clown)	Brian Hibbard
William (engineer at Akroyd's)	Dave Cameron Bache
Jack Bidwell (Akroyd's agent)	Christopher Reason
The Preacher (orthodox methodist)	Dave Cameron Bache
James Akroyd (millowner)	Nick Jensen
Mrs Akroyd (his wife)	Sally Eldridge
Mr Miller (millowner)	Gareth Williams
Major Burnside (commander of the troops)	Chris Reason
A soldier	Gareth Williams

ACT I

SCENE 1

Sunday, eighth August, eighteen forty-two. An ale house in Halifax. Wool-combers and weavers of Calderdale gathered for a social. There is a banner in the ale house reading: 'WITHOUT VOTES WE ARE SLAVES. GIVE US THE CHARTER'. Most are Chartists. As audience enter, a medley of traditional songs is being sung, some political, some of love. The auditorium becomes the ale house. Some songs sung communally. Blackout.

JOHN, *the Weaver;* SARAH *and* JENNY, *his daughters;* PETER, *a Weaver;* FRED, *another Weaver;* WILLIAM, *Akroyd's Engine Man;* ELSIE CARTER, *are present.*

Enter TINKER CLOWN *wheeling his cart. The cart has various pans, pieces of metal, the tools of his trade on it.*

Clown In comes I. Good evening one and all. (*He sings the first two verses of his song.*)
>I am a jester.
>North south east and wester
>I follow the travelling fairs
>A seasoned old grafter.
>Jokes music and laughter
>A song and a dance are my wares.
>I can see right through the rich man's disguise
>The greed and the sadness that live in his eyes.
>I turn the world upside down
>I am your travelling clown.
>
>I am a reveller
>A digger a leveller.
>I measure the short and the tall
>The lord and the peasant
>The past and the present.
>Who's rising and who's going to fall
>What lasts forever and what fades away
>What's coming to pass and what's going to stay.
>I turn the world upside down
>I am your travelling clown.

Right, here we are in the Calder Valley. Up there is Calderwike, an old-fashioned village where sweet flowers still scent the air; just above Halifax, here, which stinks. It's handloom weavers and combers live in

Calderwike, and Monday week they'll be holding their annual Fair and Feast Day, and that's why I'm here. This is hand made and all. Do you like it? That's my trade-mark. Journeying Tinker and travelling clown. (*Jangles his pans. Sings final verse.*)

> I am a tinker
> A crafty hoodwinker.
> I carry good news on my cart.
> I'll swap your sadness
> For laughter and gladness
> I'll even mend your broken heart.
> I see a new world that's hidden from view
> And if you look hard enough you'll see it, too.
> I turn the world upside down
> I am your travelling clown.

I'll tell you a story before I go. It's eighteen forty-two. England. The new workshop of the world, where a million hands lie idle. England. Where our masters have a million fine coats hanging dusty in their stores, while a million weavers can't afford just one coat to wear. England, where everyone is free, but no working people have the vote. Property is private and every Englishman's home is his landlord's. England. Eighteen forty-two. A far-fetched story of home-spun truth.

Activity in the ale house resumes.

Reprise of 'A Drop of Good Beer'.

Elsie Carter (*holding baby, to audience*) Thank you. Right, now, they've asked me to introduce tonight's entertainment which is given by the Calderwike and District Chartist Society. My name is Elsie Carter and I work here in Halifax at Akroyd's mill. But I live up in Calderwike – and I'm treasurer of the Chartist Society there. So if you want to know anything more about us you can allus get me on mill steps feeding time. Oh . . . this is Hannah. She's me third. She's lovely. Folks keep saying I ought to get wed, but I say that'd just be another mouth to feed. Now then, Calderwike Chartists are going to do a little play for us tonight. Well . . . that is . . . some of us are . . . not me. What's it called, John?

John We're doing our version of 'St George and the dragon'.

Elsie How long's it last for?

John About five or ten minutes.

Elsie Right. So I've great pleasure in introducing Calderwike . . .

Peter Elsie. Wait a minute. Fred hasn't got his head on yet.

Elsie What? Oh. He'd be late for his own funeral that one.

Peter Right. He's ready.

Elsie Introducing – Calderwike Chartist Society in 'St George and the Dragon'!

The play begins.

Peter Let me introduce to you our characters so bold,
Our heroine 'Hardworking' is a character of gold.
She represents the people. There's none to us so dear.
So please, when e'er you see her raise a might cheer.

Enter JENNY.

Our villain's Mr Millgrind, a man of infinite greed
Who for the sake of money, bairns to the flames would feed.
He has no care for common folk, the likes of me and you
So when you see him coming, let's hear you hiss and boo.

Enter JOHN.

And thirdly there's our hero, St George, the Chartist – me
Three cheers for him . . . (*Shouts of 'Gerroff'*.) . . . and maybe he
will set Hardworking free.
Lastly, there's the dragon . . . (*Enter* FRED *with a dragon's head
on.*) . . . whose temperament will unfold
Sometimes he's friendly . . . (*Gesture.*) . . . sometimes fierce . . .
(*Gesture.*) . . . depends who's in control.
Now dragon's name's Machinio and here's the reason why.
Hardworking and Machinio, together side by side
Would weave the finest linen or spin the finest thread.
They got on well together though they never shared a bed
And one dark night Hardworking slept and dreamt of Market
Day . . .

Jenny When I will sell the cloth we've made for a handsome price, I pray.
So I can buy good food and drink and a ribbon for my hair,
Which I will wear next week at the great St Monday Fair.

Peter But as she slept, in Millgrind crept . . . (*Enter Millgrind. Boos.*) . . .
and stole Machinio away
And locked him in a factory and fed him night and day.

John For if I feed Machinio, the more work will he do
And I will become richer as poorer will grow you. (*Pointing to*
HARDWORKING *and then to audience.* JOHN *cackles, audience
boos?*)

Peter He harnessed him and drove him hard by water and by steam.
Dragon turned to monster, Millgrind built his dream.
Meanwhile, our poor Hardworking, stripped of her helpmate . . .

Jenny I am on the verge of starving, I am begging for my plate.

John If you're on the verge of starving, for a pittance you can tend
The needs of my Machinio . . . I'll make you scrape and bend.

Jenny The mill bell rings at five o'clock. I've got to be on time.
For Millgrind tells me . . . For Millgrind tells me . . .

Sarah C'mon, Dad.

John	Prompt!
All	If you're late!
John	If you're late, you'll have to pay a fine.
Peter	And the monster grew quite hideous, his appetite was such,
	That nothing could satisfy his insatiable lust.
	His nostrils belched with smoke and fumes, poisonous to the lungs,
	But he produced in quantity, the cloth came out in tons.
Jenny	I work for fourteen hours a day and dare not make a slip
	For standing at my shoulder is Millgrind with his stick.
	Machinio will eat me up if I get too close to him.
	His mighty jaws and grinding teeth will tear me limb from limb.
	I used to work in my own time and I was well rewarded.
	Now I belong to Millgrind, I am used, abused, defrauded.
Peter	The story seems quite desperate, Hardworking's fate seems sealed.
	When along came St George the Chartist and to her he appealed:
	'Do you wish to free yourself from monster dragon, Machinio?'
Jenny	But how?
Peter	She cried . . .
Jenny	Without him I cannot earn a beanio.
Peter	'The problem's Mr Millgrind, he who's in control.
	Today he'll break our backs, tomorrow break our soul.
	We've got to get Machinio from out his evil hands.
	Then we'll tame the dragon. These are our demands.'

The People's Charter.

Peter	Thus spake the noble Chartist, Hardworking listened hard.
Jenny	Unless we act together, the whole plan will be marred.
Peter	The very next day Hardworking from the factory stayed away.
Jenny	No more work. From now on it's a national holiday.
Peter	Until we get the charter, the dragon idle lies.
	Millgrind's getting frightened. Tears come to dragon's eyes.
	So how will end this sorry tale, will Hardworking see the day
	When she controls Machine again and Millgrind fades away?
	Or will Machine consume her as machines are wont to do?
	The answer to this problem is up to me and you. (*Bows, etc.*)
John	Thank you very much. Now I'd like to ask you to come to the Calderwike Fair next week to see our next great production which is to celebrate Peterloo. It's called 'St Monday and the Dragoons'. Now, don't go away, Peter here is going to say a few more words.
Peter	Thank you, thank you! Now then. Like the play says, it's up to me and you if anything's to be done about the present state of things. As you know. There's thousands of us, destitute and starving for want of work in this valley. And thousands more, men, women and children, working sixty to seventy hours a week for a pittance. If this is to be changed, and our voice heard, we must have the charter, we must have the vote.

Now, at our next meeting on Tuesday night, the Calderwike and District Chartist Society will elect a delegate to the National Convention in Manchester. It's important that every working man and woman turn up for that meeting, for it may be that one day this convention, elected by ordinary working folk, may become the People's Parliament itself. Because if that load of jumped up lawyers, employers and landlords in Westminster don't give us our rights, we will set up a People's Power and take them for ourselves. The meeting will be here, eight-thirty sharp, Tuesday night. Make sure you come. Thank you.

SARAH *and* WILLIAM *are sat together.*

Jenny Did you like it?

Sarah It was great. Wasn't she, William?

William Yes . . . You took a really good part, lass. Your dad were great, weren't he? When he remembered his words.

Sarah Ooh, that's a nice bit of ribbon, our Jenny, can I try it?

Jenny Oh, no. I'm keeping this. You've got a fellah already.

Sarah I have not.

Jenny Watch her, William, she'll break your heart!

John (*bringing a drink for* JENNY) Jenny lass, here you are, get a hold of this. (WILLIAM *and* SARAH *start whispering.*)

Jenny Only a half?

John I can hardly afford that. It's enough for you.

Jenny William bought our Sarah a pint!

John Ah, well, our Sarah's got big ideas. (*Sees whisper.*) Eh, if you've got owt fit to hear, say it out loud, lad, and if it's not, keep it to yourself.

William (*caught out*) Oh. (*Standing.*) Good evening, Mr Greenwood . . . I er . . . was just saying . . . I thought you were very good in the play . . . It were very professional . . .

John Met with your approval, did it, lad? You'll be coming to the meeting then?

William No, I don't think so. It's not my sort of thing. We've got a lot of work on at the mill at moment putting in new machines. They're fantastic. Latest thing. From Palmer's in Bradford . . .

Sarah William!

John Well, I'm glad somebody's got plenty of work. One man's poison, another man's meat.

William I didn't mean . . . I . . . er. Can I get you another?

John No thanks, lad, this'll do me. So they're fantastic are they . . . Mr Akroyd'll be well pleased.

William Aye, he is. (*Pause.*) Mr Greenwood, I don't know anything about Chartists and such, I'm just a mechanic, right, and what I do know is steam power has come for good. You can't stand in the way of progress. That's where I didn't agree with your play . . .

John You must be about only one who didn't, lad. Look at folk here, look at the state of 'em. Time was everyone of 'em had a decent set of clothes and a full belly. You could earn thirty shillings a week for hand weaving or combing. Now since mill started I'll be lucky if I can earn eight and six working by hand. Why? My cloth's just as good and I work just as hard, but eight and six is all I can make. Is that progress? If it is, you and me are talking a different language.

William I'm talking about the future, Mr Greenwood, machines'll make the future . . .

John Well, I don't live in the future, lad. I'm here and now, and I don't fancy it one bit. But no doubt Mr Akroyd pays you well to look after his engines, like I said. One man's poison, another man's meat.

William You think you'd be better off if mills weren't running? 'Cos Sarah and Jenny'd be hard pushed to find owt else. Akroyd brought work to this valley, and new power looms'll mean even more.

John You want progress, lad? Then give us yer engines and we'll mek 'em spin and weave a shorter workin' day and bread for all of us. But Akroyd? He's a bastard who'll screw every last penny out of you, her, and every other bugger that works for him. You're just slaves, that's what you are . . .

William You're exaggerating . . .

John Slaves. Clock in. Clock out. Do this, do that. You've got no say. Where's your bloody pride, lad? You've got none.

Sarah Ssh, Dad.

John Don't tell me to ssh. You're as bad as he is. If I had my way you'd not be working at mill.

Sarah We'd blooming starve if I didn't.

John Don't you back chat me, my lass, or you'll get off home.

Sarah I'll do as I want.

John Oh, aye.

Sarah We were just enjoying ourselves 'till you started stirring.

John Stirring?

Sarah I came here to have a good time, not argue about blooming politics!

John I'll do more than stir it, lass. You're too clever by half.

Sarah Am I?

John You're getting as common as rest of them mill girl sluts in Halifax. You can back-slavver all you like down there but when you're up here, you'll show some respect to your father.

CLOWN *enters with clattering cart.*

Clown In Comes I! Eh up, there. Give me some room. Clear the way there. Let the dog see the rabbit.

Group breaks up. Exits.

Clown (*sings*) Bring your tins and your kettles, your pans made of metal,
I'll mend 'em and make 'em like new. (*Speaking, clattering pans.*)
> Hear ye, hear ye. Next Monday, a grand St Monday fair. Feasting
> and festivities the whole day long.
> Welcome, one and all to the great annual feast day on the green.
> At Calderwike, next Monday, August sixteenth.
> Come, one and all. Everything and anything can happen at the fair.
> When the people get together. Make sure that you're there.

(*Sings reprise of earlier song.*)

> I'll swap your sadness
> For laughter and gladness
> I'll even mend your broken heart.
> I see a new world that's hidden from view
> And if you look hard enough you'll see it, too.
> I turn the world upside down
> I am your travelling clown.

Methodist Preacher appears.

Preacher Turn, brothers and sisters. Turn ye from this idleness and wasteful
pleasure. Today I want to give each of you a warning: beware. Beware
the contagion of these Alehouse fleshpots. There is death in these
honeyed-pots of pleasure. Remember that you are God's people: of his
Government there will be no end. Be upright, honest, industrious and
methodical in all your ways. And take care that ye despise all murmurers
and complainers. Infidel Chartists, revolutionaries, yes, you there, you
know of whom it is I speak . . . yes. The Lord will cut down such filthy
dreamers.
> As for those who have already fallen, repent. Show the lord, the
pain and anguish in your heart and he will bless you. This Monday
evening we shall hold our own Holy love feast, when all blushing
sinners can take pleasure in coming to the Lord . . . Like James Tremble
there, who last year knelt in that very pew, and though the enemy
raged and rolled about him like a flood, he prayed. The more he prayed,
the more his distress and burden increased. Till finally, twisting and
writhing, his heart pounding, the sweat running from him, he felt what
no tongue can ever describe, a moment of deliverance, that sprang
through his whole frame, a burst of ecstasy – yes, he had come – to
the Lord.
> We shall now sing hymn Number Thirteen in the words of Charles
Wesley:
> > Come Oh my guilty brethren come
> > Groaning beneath your load of sin.
> > His bleeding heart shall make you room
> > His open side shall take you in.

Sing and be joyful in the Lord's pleasure.
Clown He kills me that bloke, he really does.

They exit.

SCENE 2

Outside on the way home to Calderwike from Halifax. The same night.

Enter Sarah and Jenny

Sarah He treats me like a kid.
Jenny Why? What did he say to you?
Sarah Oh usual thing, he's forever interfering. Hang on, Jenny, I'm bursting.
Jenny Can't you wait, Mam said we'd got to save it for the washing.
Sarah Hard luck, Oooh, that feels better.

SARAH *squats to piss.*

Jenny You've set me off now. Oh Heck. Ahhh!!

JENNY *squats to piss.*

Sarah Just 'cos William didn't like his rotten play. That's what it was.
Jenny Didn't he? What was wrong with it?
Sarah You know William, he thinks Dad and Chartist lot are wasting their
  time . . .
Jenny He said that did he? Serves him right then. Waste of time. I'd've done
  more than shout at him.
Sarah He talks a lot of sense.
Jenny A load of rubbish. What was he whispering to you about, anyway?
Sarah Not telling!
Jenny Ooh! Fancy you won't tell yer sister, eh? Right then . . .
Sarah All right. Promise to keep quiet?
Jenny Yes, go on?
Sarah He's got me a new job.
Jenny Where?
Sarah On new power looms.
Jenny Power looms! Sarah, Dad'll go spare.
Sarah I don't see why.
Jenny You know very well why.
Sarah I don't see how it makes any odds. I've worked in spinning shed long
  enough. It's same difference. He sent us to mills in't first place.
Jenny Spinning's one thing, but weaving! You can't, Sarah. Akroyd's
  power looms'll put Dad and Mum out of work.
Sarah If I don't do it somebody else will.
Jenny When do you start?
Sarah Next week.

Jenny How much will you get?

Sarah About three shillin' a week more.

Jenny That's good. At least you can buy our mam some soap for't washing.

John (*off*) Let me in, Soldier, let me in.

Jenny It's Dad.

Sarah Don't say owt to him. I'll tell him in me own good time.

Jenny All right.

John I demand an audience.

Jenny He's ravin' away to himself. Come on. Shh! (*They hide.*)

Enter JOHN *on his way home. Drunk.*

John I'd go in there and I'd say to Queen Victoria, 'Oi. Gerroff that throne young lass and come down here. I've got a bone to pick with you.' No messing, I would, I would.

Then she'd stutter, 'cos she'd be nervous like. She'd see I'd got my mad up and she'd threaten to fetch her Albert. 'Bring him,' I'd say. 'Bring him. I don't care. I'm not frit.' So he'd arrive and say, 'What do you want, my man?', and I'd say, 'I've come to settle national debt.' He'd say, 'And just how do you propose to do that,' and I'd reply, 'Well, you can take this for a start.' And I'd give him one, just like that. I'd grab him by the throat and I'd shake him. Then I'd turn him upside down and bang his head on the throne. Then Victoria would scream. So I'd do it again, but harder – bang, bang, bang. And she'd threaten me, 'If you don't stop I'll have you put in the tower.' So I'd toss him aside – just like that – and I'd turn to her and look her straight in the eye and say: 'Steady on, lass. Steady on, your majesty. Remember what we did to Charles the First. Don't lose your head.' (*Laughs.*)

And before she could straighten her tiara the doors would burst open, and hundreds of Chartists would storm the palace, throwing their green caps in the air and crying, 'Long live the people's charter,' and they pick me up and hold me high upon their shoulders crying, 'Speak, John Greenwood' and I'd say ... I'd say ...

Sarah⎫
Jenny⎬ Prompt.

JOHN *exits.* SARAH *and* JENNY *exit.*

Bridge music from 'Knocker Upper Song'.

SCENE 3

The Greenwood's home. A weaver's cottage in Calderwike. The same night. The cottage is small and sparse.

MARY GREENWOOD *and* DOROTHY, *her third daughter, are in the room, inspecting a roll of cloth.*

Dorothy Yes . . . Mrs Akroyd, she fainted clean away.

Mary Law me! What's up with her then? She's not expectin' again, is she?

Dorothy Well, if she was, she isn't now, not after me and Alice had finished with her.

Mary You and Alice? Whatever were you up to?

Dorothy Oh, it was all in the day's work, like. See, she called us up to her room, and she's standing there in this white chimmy thing – just got out of the bath she had, do you know she has a bath twice a week? With soap.

Mary Never.

Dorothy It's right. And the smell, like real lavender. Anyway . . . 'Come along, Dotty,' she says, she always calls me Dotty, I don't know why, 'Come along, Dotty, and help me on with my corsette.'

Mary A corsette? Whatever's that then?

Dorothy It's French.

Mary Eh?

Dorothy It sort of went all round her middle 'ere, and from 'ere to 'ere, with laces up the side. But you've never seen such a palaver. She had Alice on one side and me on the other, pulling and 'eaving to get it tight . . . I felt like old Jackson, saddlin' a horse and she was holdin' her breath, goin' redder and redder, and the more we pulled, the redder she went . . . till she ended up wi' a waist like a whippet, bosoms like prize marrows, and a face like a beetroot . . . it was then she fainted . . . I were in stitches but Alice were frit to death, she thought we'd done for her.

Mary Too bad you didn't.

Dorothy She says it's the latest fashion. And I must say, she did look lovely.

Mary Whatever next? Bloody barmy. If she wants a thinner waist, she should stop feeding her face and get some work done.

Dorothy You don't understand, Mam. Mrs Akroyd's a lady.

Enter SARAH *and* JENNY *singing 'If it wasn't for the work of the Weavers'.*

Mary You two are in fine voice . . . where's your father?

Sarah Oh, he's coming.

Jenny He's as tipsy as a wheelbarrow.

Mary Oh, aye.

Jenny Well, nearly.

Mary Did your play go all right, love?

Jenny Yeah . . . it were a really good night. Everybody were there; even William, Engine Man from Mill, but he were too interested in Sarah to watch play.

Sarah Don't fib.

Jenny (*to* MARY) True.

Sarah You've got it all done then, Mam?

Mary Aye, near enough. Dorothy gave me a hand, didn't you, love? Fill us me pipe, love, will you?

Dorothy Right, Mam.

Exit DOROTHY.

Enter JOHN *with shit on his boot.*

John Hello love. Uhhh! Look what I've brought in. That bloomin' midden heap ought to be shifted down to bottom. It's that lot from Ovenden, dirty buggers.

Jenny Did you fetch Prince Albert with you, an' all, Dad. (*Girls giggle.*)

John No, but I fetched this. (*He has* JENNY's *ribbon.*)

Jenny Oh. (*Notices she's lost it.*) Oh, Dad, thank you.

John Tie it on tight or you'll lose it for good. (*Passes boot to* SARAH. *To* MARY.) How are you getting on? Nearly finished! I'll have to get cracking tonight: Jack Bidwell'll be around for it tomorrow. On village green twelve o'clock prompt with his little book in his hand. 'Be there on the dot or you'll be forgot.' (DOROTHY *returns. To* DOROTHY.) Ow's things down at the lord and master's house?

Dorothy Fine, Dad. Alice is leaving next month, so Mrs Akroyd's making me her maid. Better than kitchen.

John Very grand I'm sure.

Sarah Here y'are, Dad. (*Returns cleaned boot.*)

Mary So they like the play, our Jenny says.

John Aye. We're doing one again next week at fair. It went well, didn't it?

Jenny Yeh.

John Got folk talking.

Mary What did they say?

John One bloke talking to me said, he thought the end should have more of a message, like, but most said it had come over well, except for that Engine Man from Akroyd's. But he's as thick as two short planks.

Sarah He is not. He spoke his mind, that's all.

John And I suppose you agree with him, do you?

Sarah I might. But he knows what he's talking about. You were just shouting at him; I was right embarrassed.

John Oh, I'm sorry! Embarrassed you, did I?

Sarah Yes.

John Well, you ought to be more careful of the company you keep lass.

Sarah It's my business who I choose to sit with. I didn't ask you to interfere.

Mary Steady on, Sarah.

Sarah He's always getting at me. I'm fed up of him.

John And I'm fed up of your cheek. Get it straight, lass, as long as you live under my roof, you do as I say.

Sarah Why should I? I earn as much as you do. I don't see why I have to be ruled by you.

John Don't you!

Mary Sarah, I've told you before, you're getting too uppety by far.

Sarah You know I'm right. That's what it is. I bring in more than he does and he can't stand it. That's why he's getting at me!

John I've fed and clothed you and put roof over your head for years lass and don't you forget it. If you don't like it, you know what you can do . . .

Sarah And maybe I will. (*He scoffs.*) You can laugh . . . but I'll be getting enough next week. I'll live on me own . . . get out of here . . .

John Next week. What's happening next week then?

Jenny Sarah!?

John Come on, let's have it. Sarah!? Jenny!?

Sarah I've got work on the new power looms.

Mary Sarah, you can't have.

Sarah It's three shillings a week more, Mam. I . . . we need the money.

John I can't believe it. My own daughter. Those machines ruin us. You know that, don't you?

Sarah If I didn't do it somebody else would.

John Akroyd's out to break us and you're doing his dirty work.

Sarah Well, at least, I'll be bringing money in instead of mooching about here weaving cloth nobody wants anymore.

Mary Don't talk to your father like that.

Sarah I'm never right. I'll work where I like and he'll not rule me.

John I see. I think I'll go upstairs and make myself useful then.

He goes.

Dorothy Well, I hope you're satisfied. What did you have to go and say all that for?

Sarah Don't you start. I only told the truth. He's just so old-fashioned.

Jenny But it's his trade, Sarah, he's been doing it all his life.

Sarah I can't help it if hand-weavin's finished. Why won't he admit it? Why go on at me?

Mary When you've been through all he has, maybe you'll understand why he's like he is. He's always been his own man, he won't give that up to no one. And he's always earnt his own keep.

Jenny So has Sarah, Mam. She's only doing it for the extra money.

Sarah I've worked in't spinning-shed since I were knee high. He can't blame me. He sent us there in first place!

Mary Not by choice he didn't, Sarah. Spinning were different. It were good for us hand-weavers. More yarn, more work coming in. But these new power looms, they're driving down our piece rates to nothin'.

Dorothy But he's got to face it, Mam, it's the same for you but you're not sulking about it.

Mary He's not sulking. He's burnin' inside. And he's not the only one. There's thousands feel like him. We've worked all our lives in the trade. Akroyd comes in, and he's takin' everything. He owns the wool, the yarn, the cloth and pretty soon he'll own all the looms. Our tools locked in his mills, and when that's done he'll own us, from start to finish. There's thousands feel like me and your father. They haven't shown it yet, not all of them, but it's coming, don't doubt it, it'll come.

Enter CLOWN.

Clown   The people are asleep.
They've been asleep for ages . . .
There's your snorer . . . (*Mime.*) . . . your restless sleeper . . .
    (*Mime.*) . . .
Your dreamer . . . good dreams . . . bad dreams.
Sleep walker, sleep talker.
But most people never wake up.
They sleep with their eyes open.
All their lives, fast asleep.
My job is to wake them up
Before they get knocked up.

SCENE 4

Two areas are required – The mill and the weaver's cottage.

'SONG OF THE KNOCKER UPPER'

Dream weary people while you may.

Night stains the land with darkening skies
The world creeps off to bed
Lays down its weary head
And floats upstream.
Sleep bathes the sorrow in your eyes
Your drowsy slumber brings
Peace from your sufferings
And you can dream of a brand new day
When you will wake up smiling.
The sun will rise above
A world made beautiful with love.

Bang bang the knocker upper is coming to get you.
Bang bang the knocker upper is coming to get you.

Oh it's so cold in here
Outside it's wet
Oh it's so dark in here
The day hasn't started yet.
You don't want to
But you've gotta get up
'Cos the man with the big stick's gonna knock you up.

JENNY *and* SARAH *appear on stage, shivering in the cold dawn. They hug each other for warmth. The mill hooter sounds. They leave for work.*

MARY *is mixing bread.* JOHN *is looking at wildflowers.*

John Moon carrot, blue bugle . . . beautiful that, isn't it, Mary . . . fantastic names, eh? I found some wild thyme down bankside wood.

Mary Wild thyme! By hell, it's a long time since I had a wild thyme.

John You should have come down to pub last night, love.

Mary Oh, aye, and that cloth would have finished itself I suppose?

John Here's one for our lass, 'Creeping Jenny'. Just right for her Mary. Eh? Did I tell you I caught her creeping in turned ten o'clock t'other night. Out with some fellah, I'll bet.

Mary She's growing up fast, John. There's plenty ready to court her, she's a pretty lass.

John Aye. Well, you know what they say, courting and wooing means dallying and doing.

Mary You should know that! She's got her head screwed on, don't you worry.

John Here's one for our Sarah . . . 'Dragon's Teeth'.

Mary You're gonna have to go a lot more steady on her, John. She's not a bad lass.

John She's wilful, Mary, bloody wilful. I don't know where she gets it from.

Mary I do.

John I should have clipped her ear.

Mary Oh, that'd help things a lot, John. She used to be your favourite when they were little. You always had her wind your bobbins for you, not Dorothy or Jenny. You doted on her. She were a right little madam then, but you loved her for it.

John High spirits in a lass is one thing, but she's picking this up from Mill. You know as well as I do what goes on down there. Young girls all in together. Overseers oggling at 'em all day. I learnt decency and respect at home, working by the loom wi' me father and mother and that's where they should be.

Mary It's not like that anymore, John. It's not easy for Sarah and Jenny either, you know. Sarah's strong headed. And she needs to be, working in mills . . .

John She's stubborn, Mary. She wouldn't help us out wi' that play would she? Not our Sarah. She's got other ideas.

Mary She's got a mind of her own and now she's a grown woman you don't like her using it.

John Our Jenny's a mind to herself but she's not like it.

Mary She's nowt to be stubborn about. Our Sarah's taking up with William, that's what's irking you isn't it, John.

John He thinks he knows it all. A right Billy Bighead. Leading her on with his bloody daft ideas about progress. I don't know what she sees in him.

Mary He's a good looking fellah. He's got a bonny face. What do you think I saw in you? The people's charter? He's a handsome lad.

John Handsome is as handsome does. Have a look at this flower, Mary. Found it down by the mill this morning.

Mary Oh, that's pretty. Nice colour. What is it?

John It's a catchfly. Here, smell it. Nice in't it? When it's opened out the scent draws any passing creature to it – once they're inside it closes round trapping 'em – or so people say. I've never seen one this colour before. Could be a discovery. Does it remind you of anything, Mary? It looks like a Sweet William.

Mary Oh, aye, it does a bit.

John I think that's what I'll call it – Sweet William Catchfly.

They exit. Bridge music – theme from 'Clown Song'.

SCENE 5

Monday, ninth August. Village Green in Calderwike.

JOHN, MARY, MS EDWARDS, ELSIE CARTER *and* PETER *sit holding their 'pieces', 'frozen' in conversation.*

Clown The handloom weavers of Calderwike are buzzing with the news that Akroyd's mill has started weaving by steam.

Hubbub of outrage from assembled weavers.

John Look, he's got us by the short and curlies. We can't match him, he'll turn it out at twice the speed of hand, I tell you.

Clown Mr Akroyd's agent, Jack Bidwell, is expected, his cart tumbling up the hill. He's coming to collect his master's pieces from the outworkers.

> In Comes I.
> Hear ye! Hear ye!
> Grand Fair in Calderwike August sixteenth.
> Festivities and Feasting.
> Are you coming to the fair folks?

All Aye, we'll be there.

Clown (*juggling apples*) One and one is three. All things being equal. (*Throws.*) Food for thought. A riddle, right. If a merchant buys three apples at one penny each and sells them to a poor man for two pence each, what should he get?

Bidwell (*off*) Bring out your cloth, bring out your wool.

John Ah, here he is, creeping Jack Bidwell.

They form a queue with their 'pieces'.

Bidwell Right then, let's have your pieces. (EDWARDS, *woman, hands piece.*) On time as usual, Mrs Edwards. Let's have a look then. (*Examines.*)

Ms Edwards It's a good piece, Bidwell. Tight up, not a break in it. There's not a closer weft, you know me.

Bidwell Indeed I do, but I've said it before and it bears repeating, take owt on trust and you'll soon go bust, a full length is it . . . aye . . . right. Then that's seven shillings.

Ms Edwards Seven shillings? Oh, no. Eight shillings and sixpence, Bidwell, that's what we agreed. That's the rate.

Mary Come on, Jack Bidwell. We haven't got time for your chinnanigans, pay up and let's get on.

Bidwell Mr Akroyd has stated. Seven shillings. As of today. That is the rate. (*Consternation.*) He can't afford any more than that. Trade is down and facts are facts. (*They confer, then disperse.*) Come on, there's no-one else'll buy your cloth, or give you yarn to weave!

Peter Are you on the fiddle again, Bidwell?

John You tell me when he isn't.

Bidwell It's Mr Akroyd's word, Greenwood. Take it or leave it. My instructions are, them as wants to go on working, he'll pay seven shillings.

Mary That's bloody blackmail.

Bidwell Take your choice, those that want seven shillings can collect their fresh yarn from the mill tomorrow.

Voice We can't do it for that. I'd be paying more out for candles than I can make on seven shillings.

Bidwell I can't hang about here all day. That's the offer. Come on, they've accepted it at Midgeley.

Peter Never.

Ms Edwards You're lying, Bidwell. They're not that daft in Midgeley.

Bidwell It's true, come on. What about you Greenwood. You'll not take the new rate, I suppose, will you? Too busy with your damn Chartism and daft plays to do a good day's work.

John I'm not takin' seven shillings, Bidwell. Never.

Bidwell It'll be no great loss. There was never any quality to your work.

John I'll stuff it down your throat. Quality? You'll feel the quality of my hands, Bidwell.

Bidwell You're finished, Greenwood.

John And so are you mate. Let's have him. (JOHN *grabs him and punches.*)

Mary (*stops* JOHN) Steady on, John. Wait a minute, Peter. You don't beat a man by kicking his dog. This is only Mr Bidwell, you know him, creeping Jack Bidwell. You were a weaver once yourself, weren't you, Jack? Aye. Now he's Mr Akroyd's agent, that's all, his errand boy. Be fair. You're only doing your job, aren't you, Jack? He's only come for Mr Akroyd's pieces, that's all. Haven't you?

Shaken. He is held and gets up.

Bidwell That's right.

Mary And to deliver Mr Akroyd's messages.

Bidwell That's right.

Mary And pay out the money?

BIDWELL *hands purse.*

Mary Thank you. We'll take what's owed us, eight and six, that's all.
Bidwell What about Mr Akroyd's cloth?
Mary Mr Akroyd can have his pieces and you can take him a message an' all.
You can tell him he can stuff his seven shillings . . . and he'll get no more
work from any outworker till the old piece rate is back. Can you re-
member that, Jack? (*He nods.*) Well, in case you can't.

She and rest unroll piece and CLOWN *produces bucket and brush from cart.*
MARY *whispers to* CLOWN. *He paints.*

Peter But it's upside down.
Clown Course it's upside down – I wrote it!
Mary Well, turn it then.

They do. It says: 'The Piecemakers will fight.'

They see it. All shout it.

John (*holding* BIDWELL) There, take that to your boss Mr Bidwell. Wrap it up,
under your arm, or better still . . . (*He wraps him in the piece. Everybody
joins in.*)
Voice Let's give him a stang ride.
Voice Aye, right.
Voice Stick him on yon cart.

BIDWELL *is trussed up, decorated with wool, etc, and carried off to music
and singing 'A Stang Ride'.* CLOWN *and* MARY *are left.*

Mary Well done Tom.

Hands him his paint and brush.

Clown So you got the answer to me riddle then?
Mary Aye, he gets what he deserves.
Clown Right. And more than he expected. There'll be hell to pay.
Mary I'm glad, I'd rather have it out this way than keep going down and
down till nothing's left.
Clown Have you ever been to Manchester?
Mary A few times. Why?
Clown I was there last week, there's great rumblings. I met a man in Ashton
who said the whole of Manchester would be out before this weekend
gone.

The 'stang ride' passes again. JOHN *and* PETER *stay. The* CLOWN *joins in
and exits.*

John By, that were grand. 'The piecemakers will fight.' Well done, Mary.
But wait till Akroyd hears . . . then we'll have a fight on our hands.

We'll have to get millworkers behind us. We'll talk to Elsie.

Mary John, you know that Lancashire Chartists are organising big turnout Manchester way?

John There's been a few rumours.

Mary Aye. Well Tom were there last week. And he reckons they'll all be out by next weekend. I reckon someone ought to get over there and find out what's happening. Tell 'em what's goin' on here.

John Aye, right. Who though?

Mary Aye.

John Peter and Fred and me've got to practise for play.

Mary I fancy a good walk – brush the cobwebs away – collect a bit of wild thyme.

John Oh no, I'll go Mary. It'd be safer for a man, besides, we need you at home.

Mary That's settled then, I'm off. I'll bring you back a flower or two. Eh! Don't forget to take Elsie's kid to the mill dinner time, then you can talk to her about what's goin' off. (*Exit.*)

John Elsie's kid – hang on Mary! Oh, bloody hell. (*Exit.*)

The sound of the power loom.

SCENE 6

Monday, ninth August. Outside Akroyd's mill.
WILLIAM *sits polishing a piece of metal. Enter* CLOWN. *Power looms still heard.*

Clown Who is this man, whose name's on everybody's lips? James Akroyd, son of a handloom weaver, self-made man. What makes him tick?

Mr Akroyd enters. Listens to his power looms.

William Morning, Mr Akroyd.

Akroyd Listen to that, William. Purring along. (*Power loom sound.*) Any problems?

William No, they're fantastic efforts, Mr Akroyd. Ticking over sweetly since they put them in. They're beauties.

Akroyd There's something about cast iron? Rock solid and at the same time you get a real feel of that power turning. I remember when I saw my first engine. Over Bradford way, an enormous old cross beam pumper, a real monster. But it were the colours: coal black iron, shining brass, and white clouds of steam bursting out the piston ends, that's what stuck in my mind – beautiful's the word. What's that you've got there?

William Oh, it's just someat I'm workin' on. Trying it out. I'm not sure about it. It's a scrap bit off one of mules. I . . .

Akroyd That's all right, lad. (*Takes it, examines.*) Did you do that join?

William Yes, sir.

Akroyd A nice job. It has a feel to it, brass. (*Hands back.*) Keep at it, William. I always fancied I'd invent something brilliant when I were your age . . . polishing metal till me fingers were raw. It gets a hold of you, doesn't it?

William Yes . . . I've been at this ever since they started putting new looms in. I don't know how far it'll get.

Akroyd Nobody knows how far they'll get, when they're travelling new ground, William. Even when you're getting nowhere, you get somewhere in the end. (*Hooter.*) Keep at it, lad, and if there's any problems in loom shed, let me know right away. (*Exit* AKROYD.)

SARAH, JENNY *and* ELSIE *come out and sit for their lunch break. They are exhausted. They notice* WILLIAM.

Sarah Still polishing yer whatsit, are yer, William?

Jenny Whatever will he do when he gets it clean, our Sarah?

Sarah He'll screw it back on where it fell off . . .

William I might need a bit of help to do that.

Jenny Need a bit of spanner, do yer?

Sarah What is it then, William?

William Nothing for you.

Sarah (SARAH *takes it*) Let's have a look.

William Give it 'ere.

Sarah Eh, Jenny, bet you this is the thing that makes the mill go.

Jenny Yeah, without it the whole mill would grind to a halt. (*They are throwing it to each other, with* WILLIAM *the pig in the middle.*)

Sarah Quick, give it 'ere – I'll bury it somewhere . . .

William It's nowt of sorts. Give it back.

Jenny Not till yer tell us who's your sweetheart.

William I'll brain you. Give it 'ere.

Jenny In't he handsome when he's angry, Sarah? I couldn't 'alf fancy 'im.

Sarah Here y'are William. (*A bit annoyed with* JENNY.)

William Thank you!

Sarah Is it important?

William It's something I'm doing, that's all.

Sarah You're funny you. Yer like work don't you.

William Aye, I do – gives me a chance to think. What do you think of new looms? Beautiful, aren't they, bloody brilliant. One day I'll make someat like that.

Sarah Tha' what?

William Don't you like working them?

Sarah Oh, it's grand. Marvellous. Just like the last job, only different.

Jenny Think yerself lucky you haven't been left in the spinning shed. They've made me cover two extra machines, on top of mine. I've been running round in circles all morning.

William (*to* SARAH) If you don't like working there's only one thing to do. Find yourself a nice young man and get yerself wed.

Jenny Oh, William. I never knew you cared. Is this really happening to me – out of all these beauties you've chosen me, a young girl of sixteen.

William No, I haven't. Does she ever stop?

Sarah Yes. When she's eating. Go on, eat yer snap, our Jenny. Come on, then. What's all this about me getting wed?

William Only to the right man. He'll have to be good enough for you, mind.

Jenny That won't be difficult.

William An 'up and coming young fellah, with an eye to the future.

Jenny Up and coming. Watch him, Sarah. He's polishing his whatsit again. Up and coming . . .

Sarah Every fellah I know is down and out.

William Maybe you've not looked hard enough.

Jenny Eh up!

William You know what they say about factory girls. Make 'em your sweetheart but never make 'em your wife. That right, Sarah? Do you think you'd make a good wife?

Jenny Why don't you ask me? I've shared her bed since I was born.

Girls laugh.

William Your sister's a laugh a minute, in't she. Eh! Why don't you take up with Tom Tinker and join the fair. The Travelling Clown and the Fool from Calderwike. You'd make a fortune.

Jenny Who's a fool?

William You are. The Fool from Calderwike. Eh, Sarah?

Jenny You can talk. You know what they say. Halifax born and Halifax bred. Strong in the arm and soft in the 'ead.

Sarah Jenny!

JENNY'S SONG

Jenny (*sings*)
        I work my machine
        Clickety clack clickety clack
        Keep one eye on the bobbin
        While the shuttle shoots back.
        From six in the morning
        Till I clock off at half past nine
        And the overseer says
        That you're slacking, my girl.
        But I don't hear him shout
        'Cos I'm in another world
        Thru the hiss of the steam
        I can dream a special dream that's mine.

        You may ask why it is that I wear
        This pretty green ribbon that you see in my hair.

Well, it's not for some bright Sonny Jim
Who swears to his mates that I wears it for him
And it's not for the factory.
I wears it 'cos I got a dream I've hidden away
That nobody else can see.

Now the overseer here
He's as slippery as soap
And he never was above
Trying to steal a quick grope.
And he's old and he drinks
And he's fat and he stinks of gin
And every factory lad
Seems to think that I'm game.
Can you wonder that I think
All men are the same.
So I've left them behind
'Cos that's the state of mind I'm in.

So you may ask why it is that I smile.
It's not 'cos I think this job's worthwhile.
It's not at the thought that my life
Will be spent as some wretch of a factory boy's wife.
And it's not 'cos I think I'm free.
I wears it 'cos I got a dream I've hidden away
That nobody else can see.

In the cold dark morning
I trudge to the mill
And me clogs feel like lead.
As I struggle down the hill
Me tired legs ache
Even 'fore the day break has come.
And I work and I sweat
In the flickering light
From first thing at morning
Till last thing at night.
Another day's been
And I've never once seen the sun.

So you may ask what fills me with hope
And what I got inside that allows me to cope.
You may ask how I muddle through
On dreams anybody else would say can't come true.
You may ask how I stay alive.

> Well if it wasn't for the dream that I've got hidden away
> I don't think I'd survive.

Sarah (*to* WILLIAM *eating his sandwich*) 'Ere, give us a bit.

William Gerroff, eat your own.

Sarah Aw, go on. (*They scuffle for it.*)

Sarah Mmm, this is nice. Is it shop bought?

William No, my mother made it. Allus just right. Can you bake?

Sarah No, I can't.

William Eh?

Sarah Can you spin?

William No, but . . .

Sarah I can.

William You've been doing it all your life.

Sarah Well, how do you expect me to bake then?

William Not much point a fellah marrying you. He'd starve.

Sarah He'd not be much of a fellah then, would he?

William You're sharp, aren't you, Sarah? You know . . . I like you a lot . . .

Sarah But do you like my sister, 'cos I'm saddled with her.

William Will you walk out wi' me on Saturday – after work. (*They look at* JENNY.) Tell 'er you're working late.

Sarah Oh, she'd swallow that, I'm sure.

William Will yer?

Sarah I'll think about it. (*She goes over to* JENNY. WILLIAM *polishes again.*)

Elsie What is it you've got there, young William?

William Nowt much.

Elsie You don't get that agitated about nowt.

William Well, it's this new gadget I've thought up. You've seen new looms. How main arm shifts back and forth on side like, as Shuttle passes.

Elsie Aye.

William This piece'll attach to that and have a rod that comes out at right angles, see?

Elsie Yeah.

William And that'll be attached to a cradle.

Elsie A what?

William A cradle. Clever eh! So a woman could work loom and have her kid close by, like. It'd save you cost of a minder and having to go out to feed baby on mill steps.

Elsie Are you serious?

William Oh yeah. It'll work all right. What do you think?

Elsie Bloody marvellous. Tell you what William, you could fit a bed on t'other end and then whole family could sleep in mill. It'd save rent and travelling. Looms could go all night.

William You'll see. Some people think a lot of my ideas.

Enter JOHN *with* ELSIE's *baby, and* CLOWN *from opposite side.*

John Elsie.

Elsie John! Where's Mary. Oh, thank you. (*Takes child to feed.*)

John Gone off to Manchester. Any chance of a word with you?

William Hello, Mr Greenwood.

John How do . . .

Elsie Oh, you've met our genius before have you, John. He was just showing me his latest invention. He's gonna move our whole family into mill, aren't you, William? . . . Continuous production day and night.

John Don't mock, Elsie. This lad has got the key to the future in his hands. We're going to have machines that talk, machines that fly, wash your clothes and cook your food – they'll even have your babies for you one day.

Clown There's laughter now. But what lies behind it? Six times the workers in this mill have had their wages cut these last two years. And in all other mills around. In Staleybridge I met a man who lost his wife and four children. I saw them huddled together dead, beneath a threadbare blanket. Hard times. And worse to come.

Enter AKROYD.

Akroyd Now then, I'm not the sort of man that goes round by Bradford to get to Leeds. I'll come straight to it. You've all seen our new looms. I've sunk every penny I've got into them. Providing you work, while there's many other mills have shut down. But I've no orders on my books, and no contracts. Because trade is bad. In fact, it's terrible. So what's to be done? Now I'm a fair man. I don't want to see my hands thrown onto the parish. It's degrading, and a great burden to those of us who pay rates. James Akroyd is not a mean man. So I'm prepared to stand by you. I'm prepared to risk all in the hopes that we can pull through together. So I've decided. Nobody will lose their jobs but wages will be reduced by half penny an hour from tomorrow. If we can just get stuck in we'll weather the storm. Good day to you.

Clown Trouble at mill! (*Exit.*)

All speak simultaneously, but distinguishable.

Voice That's slave rates. I'd sooner starve than have this.

Voice We're not wearing that, job or no job, I'd tell 'em straight down the line.

Voice First us outworkers, then you lot at mill.

Voice By Christ, they're showing their colours now.

Elsie Now listen everybody, I don't know which way you're all thinking, but I say we should refuse this. Tell him straight – enough's enough! And now's the time to make a stand.

Jenny Aye. Let's turn out here and now. That'll show the bastard.

William And then where will you be. A strike'll get us nowhere. You can see by other mills in Halifax that trade is bad. Bring Akroyd down and then where will you get work? Breaking rocks at poorhouse?

Jenny Whose side are you on?

Elsie Aye. You're talking like a gaffer's man William. You don't think Akroyd cares about the likes of us do you? We work his mills for him, that's all. Give in over this and he'll know he can drive us down till we end up at poorhouse anyroad!

William Give the man a chance, will yer! I say we should send a delegation to him, with a petition signed up and agreed by us all.

Jenny (*interrupting*) Petitions are a waste of time.

William (*continuing*) With a petition showing the hardship this'll cause. He'll do right by us. You'll see.

John Dream talk, lad, if you ask me. Look here, not three months since we sent a delegate from Halifax with a petition with Charter demands on it to Parliament. Three million or more names lad. Damn thing near stretched from here to London! And what did they do? Nothing! We might as well have spat in the wind.

Sarah Well I think William's right. I say we should have a petition.

Jenny We should turn out here and now.

Sarah That's just like you, Jenny. Trying to run before you can bloody walk.

Elsie (*shutting them up*) All right. All right. We'll give the man a chance. Akroyd can have his petition, and when he don't take no heed – then we'll have a turnout. But I tell you this: there'll be turnouts all over before long – for the Charter. The day we get the Charter – that'll be the day we put paid to wage cutting once and for all!

Factory hooter, WILLIAM *starts to go.*

Hang on a minute, William. We've got to sort out your delegation. (WILLIAM *hesitates.*) Well. Who's going to take it then?

John You go, Elsie. You'd put it best.

Jenny Aye, you would.

Elsie What about you coming, William?

William No – er – I think it'd be better coming from the women.

Jenny I'll go. I'm not frit.

Elsie Right. That's settled then. We'll take it Saturday.

They all move to go. JENNY *and* WILLIAM *exit.*

John So you won't go with your sister then?

Sarah Two's enough. Besides, I'm off out on Saturday.

John Where?

Sarah That's my business.

SARAH *exits.*

Hooter goes again. ELSIE *and* JOHN *are left.*

Elsie What was it you wanted to tell me, John?

John You're not alone. He's cut piece rate for outworkers 'an all. We're in this together. But – there's talk of big turn-outs in Manchester. I can tell you more tomorrow, Mary should be back by then.

Elsie I'll get back inside, see if I can't wake some of that lot up a bit.

John Keep on at 'em, Elsie. I'll see you tomorrow.

Elsie She's in another world. Look at her.

John Good luck to her, a better place to be than here, eh, little one, a better place than here.

Exeunt all. Machine noise.

AKROYD *returns to the scene.* CLOWN *appears with* BIDWELL *in tow, wrapped up.* AKROYD *is dumbfounded.* CLOWN *unwinds* BIDWELL *so that he spins across stage revealing 'Piecemakers will fight'.* BIDWELL, *arms freed, takes the rag from his mouth.*

Bidwell Get that clown.

BIDWELL *and* AKROYD *go for him.* CLOWN *halts them in their steps.*

Clown (*to audience*) I don't know about anyone else but I could do with a pint. Back here in ten minutes, all right?

He rings his bell.

During the interval 'The Piecemakers will fight' cloth is displayed visibly on stage.

END OF ACT I

ACT II

SCENE 7

Wednesday eleventh August. A hillside on the Manchester Road. CLOWN *sits head slumped by his cart.*

John At last. I've been looking all over for you, Tom. I've brought you a pan . . . Any chance . . . What's up wi you?

Clown I got three bumps on my head.

John How did you get them?

Clown I got banjaxed.

John What happened?

Clown There I was running as fast as my bandy little legs could carry me away from Bidwell and Akroyd . . . When my groin accidentally happened to make contact with this large black boot, leaving me flat on me back looking up at this constable – who just happened to have in his hand a rather large piece of wood, which bore some resemblance to a truncheon, so quick as a flash, without really thinking about it, I tried to remove said truncheon from constable's hand with my head, while he swung his boot in again to regain his balance. Then he hit me again on the head . . . Still, I needed the sleep. Next thing I knew, I woke up in the middle of nowhere.

John He's a nasty piece of work that constable. Any chance and he's in there.

Clown I've met plenty like him travelling around – all shapes and sizes, peelers, coppers, bobbies, every name under the sun – the law. But have you noticed, it don't matter what folk call them, they always call themselves the Force – wallop.

John Aye. Mind you military are worse. Remember Peterloo, sixty thousand of us in our Sunday best. Suddenly all 'ell broke loose. The military 'dispersed' the crowd. Sixteen dead – wicked, that were. Every march or big Chartist meeting I go on now, I go prepared. (*Mimes using saucepan as gun.*)

Clown You take a saucepan with you!?

John No, I take me gun. I brought this to see if there was owt you could do at it.

Clown Let's have a look. Soon have it fixed.

Mary (*distant*) John . . . John . . .

John What . . . Who's that . . . it's Mary. (MARY *enters breathless. He hides pan behind back.*) Mary, you're back. How'd you get on?

Mary Let me get me breath. Hello, Tom.

John Any news, what's goin' on, did you meet Lancashire lot?

Mary Yes . . . Yes . . . Ooh . . . Have I got news . . . Ooh . . . 'Ere, read that. (*Takes out paper.*) You was right, Tom.

John (*reads*) Dreadful disturbances in Ashton-under-Lyne. (*Bangs pans.*) Massive turn-outs in Manchester and Stockport. (CLOWN *bangs his pans.*) Employers fear national turn-out. (*Bangs.*) Ten thousand Chartists meet on Stalybridge Moor (*Bang . . . Bang.*) Magistrates fear insurrection. (*Bangs crescendo.*) By hell. Is it right, Mary?

Mary It is that, and more. There's a plan, John, from Northern Chartists. They're organised. I've got all details. Before long they'll be coming over the top into Calder Valley.

John Into Calder Valley! A national turn out, by heck.

Mary Aye, John, that's the way it's going, and they want us to be ready. There's a hell of a lot to get done. We've got to get organised.

Clown How long?

Mary A few days maybe. They'll send word, they said.

John We'll be ready all right.

Mary It's not that easy, John. They've brought troops up, thousands of 'em, and they've been wading into crowds in Ashton.

John Aye, I'll bet. Well, they'll get more than they bargain for over 'ere.

Clown Aye.

John There's plenty'll give 'em a taste of their own medicine . . .

CLOWN *brandishes pan as gun.*

Mary Hang on. Isn't that our pan, John?

John That's . . . er, yes, love . . .

Mary Let's have a look. It's ruined. There's a hole right thro' it.

John Not ruined, love, it's only a little hole.

Mary John, it's the only one we've got!

John I'm sorry, love, I just left it – and when I came back . . .

Mary I'll do you.

John It'll mend, won't it, Tom?

Clown Let's have a look. Oh, very small. (*Sticks finger through.*) Do that in a couple of winks . . . if . . . I can just get me finger out. (JOHN *helps him.*)

Mary Pair of clowns together you are. Look, I'm going up to see Peter, straight away, John. There's a lot to get sorted.

John I'll come with you.

Mary You'd better stay and help him get his finger out. We need that pan.

(*Exits and finger is freed.*)

John Get cracking then. (*Starts tapping pan to repair.*)

Clown What's it say?

John (*reads from paper* MARY *has given him*) A speaker from the Lancashire Chartists said: 'We have planted a seed, and if you listen close, you can hear it growing. One day this land will be green with liberty. But if any come to blight the People's harvest there will be plenty of good strong blades ready to prevent them.' Too right there will be!

CLOWN *mimes using pan as gun.*

John One snag. (*Mime.*) Eh, Tom. Where do we get the lead?
Clown The Lord will provide.
John Eh?
Clown When was the last time you were in church? C'mon.

They exit.

Bridge music to indicate melodramatic suspense.

SCENE 8

Dead of night. The churchyard.

Enter JOHN, MARY, PETER *with a ladder.* CLOWN *rattles pans off.*

All Sh. Sh. Sh.
Clown Sorry.
John Come on wi' that ladder.
Peter Are you sure?
John Course I am!
Mary Will you two shut up and get on with it. (*To* CLOWN.) You keep watch at the gate. If you see owt coming, whistle.
Clown (*tries*) I can't.
Mary All right, make a signal.
Clown I'll go 'twit, twoo'. (*Very loud.*)
John What the bloody hell were that?
Mary Shhh, go on.

JOHN *and* PETER *climb onto roof.* MARY *keeps watch below.*

Peter Have you got the lever?
John Yes. (*They start cutting.*)
Peter By, it's bloody thick lead on 'ere.
John There's enough here to serve a regiment. It'll melt down lovely.
Peter You'll be a regular christian soldier wi' this in your musket.
John Aye. God on our side, and no mistake.
Mary Shh.
Peter Sorry. Roll her up, slow now. Keep it tight.
Peter Christ – it's heavy.
Clown (*off*) Twit, twoo.
Mary Quiet. There's someone coming. Keep down.
Clown (*entering*) Quick, it's the preacher.
Mary The preacher? What am I gonna do?

Clown Pray.

Mary Eh?

Clown Get down on your knees and pray. You know, 'Our father . . .' (*He exits.*)

Mary (*on her knees*) Our father that . . .

John Art . . . art.

Mary Art in heaven.

Peter Hallowed.

Mary Hallowed be thy name. Forgive us this day our . . . daily bread.

PREACHER *has entered and is listening.*

Preacher Good evening. It's Mary Greenwood, isn't it?

Mary Yes, sir!

Preacher You? Praying?

Mary Oh, sir, I'm sorry, I . . .

Preacher Do not apologise, my child. I heard noises. But to find you here, of all people, and at this hour.

Mary Oh, Reverend, I couldn't sleep. (*Gestures to* JOHN *and* PETER *to climb down.*) It's my husband.

Preacher I thought as much. Oh, I have seen him . . .

JOHN *and* PETER *freeze on ladder.*

Mary Oh, no!

Preacher Oh yes, I have seen him descending lower and lower into damnation.

Mary Oh, yes, you are right, Reverend. He wounds me to the quick, to the quick. (*Gestures to* JOHN *and* PETER.)

Preacher It is never too late to repent, Mary. You have come to the Lord's house for his help in time of troubles. You will not leave empty handed, my child.

Mary I hope not – after all the trouble . . . But I need forgiveness for my sins. Oh, God take away my sin. Take it away.

Preacher The Lord will forgive all who trespass against him.

Mary I hope so.

JOHN *and* PETER *creep off.*

Preacher But all those who despise his statutes. All those whose mouths are full of deceit, mark my words, the sword without and the terror within will destroy them.

Mary You never spoke a truer word, Reverend.

Preacher Aye. The day is coming, Mrs Greenwood. The day is coming.

He exits.

CLOWN *imitates cock crow.*

Mary Oh yes, it certainly is. The day is coming. (*Exit.*)

Bridge music. 'Jenny's Song.'

SCENE 9

Thursday, twelfth August. Dawn in Calderwike.

The CLOWN *appears. He is holding a ribbon, like* JENNY'S.

Clown The night disappears. The day is coming. My job is to wake people up before they get knocked up. But is it too late for some? (*Takes ribbon and makes it vanish.*) Now you see her, now you don't.

JENNY'S *voice is heard singing part of her earlier song. A mounting machine noise obscures her voice, builds, dominates. Silence.* GREENWOOD *family seated, silently, in background.* CLOWN *reads the Coroner's Report.*

Clown Coroner's report. The accident took place in the spinning-shed of the mill of Mr James Akroyd at seven on the morning of Thursday, August twelfth. The victim, Jennifer Greenwood, daughter of John Greenwood, handloom weaver, was attending to spinning-machines in the afore-mentioned shed. On the morning in question, she had bent down to pick up certain loose bobbins, lying under the machine, which were in the habit of becoming dislodged. To reach the bobbins she had to pass close to the moving belt which powers the machine. On this occasion, the victim's hair ribbon became entangled in the buckles, which form the belt into a loop, lifting her at great speed from the ground, carrying her upwards with the belt. In this manner, the victim's head was brought into contact with the ceiling of the shed with extreme force. It being some time before the power could be disengaged, the victim was carried round some several times, each time striking the ceiling in the above-mentioned manner. On being cut free from the belt, her head displayed multiple fractures. She was pronounced dead immediately. We interviewed the overseer in the spinning-shed who informed us that all operatives, in-cluding Jennifer Greenwood, the deceased, had been instructed not to retrieve fallen bobbins. This was the work of small children, employed specifically for this purpose. The accident is illustrative of the need for extreme care and discipline on the part of all operatives working with machinery. We consider that James Akroyd, owner, took all reasonable precautions, to ensure the well-being of his employees. We find that Jennifer Greenwood died by accidental cause.

SARAH *steps forward and sings.*

Sarah (*sings*) SARAH'S GRIEF SONG
   Listen to the death bell groaning out its toll of grief
   Sounding from the church tower up above.

Listen to the weeping as fresh dug earth is scattered
Down into the grave of the one we loved.
Listen to the grinding of the engine that's still turning
I listen for her song but she's not there.
Listen to the silence, the lonely awful silence.
My sister wore a ribbon in her hair.

She was full of life
'Allus had me laughing.
My sister's gone I can't forget her.
The flowers on the hill bloom in the summer,
I know I never will forget her.

But while the engines still turn
Working us to death,
I know my anger will burn,
As long as I have breath,
I'll never let them forget her
I'll never let them forget her,
I'll never let them forget her.

Enter PREACHER, *elevated.*

Preacher Death is come in upon us.

GREENWOODS *exit.*

Clown (*enters*) In comes I. (*Somersaults.*) Good Grief. (*To audience.*) What's up with you lot? You look like death warmed up. Cheer up it may never happen.

Preacher We are gathered here, brethren, to mourn our departed sister, Jennifer Greenwood, spinster.

Clown It has happened.

Preacher She came forth like a flower and was cut down.

Clown Funny thing about flowers. You know some people only send you flowers when you're dead. What a sense of humour.

Preacher She will be rewarded in heaven.

Clown See what I mean. She gets flowers for dying, rewards in heaven – what does she get for a living?

Preacher Since the age of five she toiled and she laboured, eating not the bread of idleness.

Clown You call that living.

Preacher Heavenly father, we mourn this your servant who has reached the end of her days.

Clown There are two ways to mourn. Some people mourn the dead, others mourn the living.

Preacher We pray for her soul.

Clown But for some people mourning is the beginning of a new day. Mourning's the time to wake up.

Preacher But heed my warning. Jennifer Greenwood was a sinner. She frequented the alehouse, she sang profane songs, she danced, she even took part in theatrical productions. Remember my words, 'There is death in those honeyed pots of pleasure.'

Clown Honeyed pots of pleasure. Funny way to describe a mill.

Preacher Brethren, turn your faces from idleness and frivolity and the light amusements of trivial fools. There is one such come upon us, a rascally tinker, a contemptible clown who struts like a crow in the gutter, the Devil in a patchwork shirt.

Clown Sounds familiar.

Preacher The Devil glints in his eye (CLOWN *winks.*) The Devil beckons in his voice. See how the work of the Lord bears me witness. Behold the wrath of the Lord (*Thunder and lightning.*) See the heavens open. Vengeance is mine saith the Lord – I will rain down destruction on all who keep company with fools – on your own head be it. (CLOWN *tips pan of water over preacher's head.*) The roof – my God – it's gone.

Clown This time we raised the roof. Next time we'll bring the bloody house down.

Reprise of 'Sarah's Song'.

SCENE 10

Saturday, fourteenth August. Afternoon on Shibden Head.

WILLIAM *and* SARAH *have just climbed to the top.*

Sarah By, it's a grand view from up here. In't it tiny. Hello, everybody. I'm up here enjoying missen. I'm glad I came now.

William Bradford's over there. (*Points left.*) And Leeds yonder. Halifax down there. (*Points right.*) And 'ere's Calderwike just above it. (*Points centre.*)

Sarah Oh aye. There's church.

William In't that your 'ouse?

Sarah Where?

William Over to 'left o'th church.

Sarah That big place! That's Hollin Hall, silly.

William Nay. Between hall and 'church.

Sarah I can on'y see fields.

William Look, down a bit. (*He's holding her and pointing.*) Now, see all them little houses.

Sarah Yes.

William Yours is one o' them in't it?

Sarah Third one along. I've never been up here before, William. It makes everything seem right different don't it? I wish our Jenny could've seen this.

William You see over by Shelf ironworks there. All them cottages down in t' bottom. That's where we live. You can just see it. And that's mill wi' big chimney, see.

Sarah I can't believe she's dead. It don't make sense. I feel like I want to grab her arm and bring her up here, 'Come up here, our Jen, come and see what it looks like from up here.'

William It's hard I know, Sarah. Don't.

Sarah I can't forget. She said it herself. 'He'll work us to death.' She said it.

William Try not to think about it, Sarah.

Sarah I didn't listen to her. I was too busy thinking about meself. I weren't bothered about her an' Elsie and rest of em . . . Why did it have to appen to her? Why?

William What's past is past. It's no good grieving, Sarah. Come on. Sit down.

Sarah We used to go for walks wi' our dad when we were little. He were always discovering flowers and makin' up names for 'em. He's crazy about flowers and things. We'd get im right needled sometimes. Our Jenny picked this flower once . . . 'Oo smell this', she said, 'It's called "Sarah's armpit".' Allus had me laughing . . . I just can't forget it. I'm sorry William, I just can't.

William It's all right. My dad were killed in ironworks when I were a kid. Slipped! It's a bloody mess down there, Sarah. Filth and dirt. Look you can see it settling over them houses . . . Folks walking around coughing and spluttering. Not fit for rats. But look over there. It's the railway they're building. When it's finished it'll take only two hours to get to Manchester.

Sarah It took our mam two days there and back.

William The world's getting smaller, Sarah. Every morning I look at that railway. I see how much further it's got, since day before. 'Cos when it's finished, I'm off.

Sarah What d'yer mean?

William There's no future here. Too many bad memories. I've got a trade that's in demand. I want to move on.

Sarah What about your folks?

William Like I said, too many bad memories. I've got prospects, Sarah and I want to make the most of them. But I don't want to go alone. Will you come with me?

Sarah What? Just up and leave me mam and dad, our Dorothy, everyone? With what's happened?

William If you marry me, you'll not want. You won't have to work down there any more. We can get out of this place and start afresh.

Sarah You never start afresh.

William Sarah, listen. We're living in a world that's changing fast. It's full of pain but it's full of promise. There's some that'll suffer, but there's others'll make the most of it. What do you want, Sarah, the pain or the promise.

Sarah You talk as though I've got no choice. It's all right standing on top 'ere, pretending it's nowt to do with me. But it's us down there, William. We're in it up to our bloody necks.

William We don't have to stay in it. We can escape, get away.

Sarah You don't escape from it by running away. You don't leave memories behind. You leave your own folks, fighting it without you.

William So you don't want to marry me . . .

Sarah You didn't ask me that.

William I did.

Sarah You asked me to leave Calderwike.

William If you loved me, you'd leave.

Sarah If you loved me, you'd stay.

William (*picks up dandelion*) Perhaps I'll stay . . . (*Blowing dandelion.*) She loves me, she loves me not, she loves me . . .

Sarah That's not what you do with it. (*Picks up another.*) One o'clock, two o'clock, three o'clock, four o'clock.

William Rubbish.

Sarah I bet you it's four o'clock.

William (*takes out his watch*) Will you give me a kiss if you're wrong? It's ten minutes to five. (*Starts to kiss her.*)

Sarah William, I've got to meet Elsie at five. I'm going with her to Akroyd's wi' that petition.

William Leave it, Elsie can take it on her own, we were just gettin' comfy.

Sarah I've got to do it. I owe it to Jenny. Come with us, William.

William Me. Don't talk daft!

Sarah Why not? It was your idea in the first place. Why shouldn't you come?

William Because I've got more sense!

Sarah But you suggested it.

William Yes. Because if Elsie'd had her way, we'd have all been out on the cobbles by now. Let it be, Sarah. She's mouth enough on her own. You're well out of it.

Sarah You might be, but I'm not. You're selfish. You only care about yourself, don't you?

William Sarah!

Sarah Well, you can stay by yourself and play with your dandelion. I'm going. (*Exit.*)

Bridge music – 'Akroyd Song' theme.

SCENE 11

The same evening. Back of AKROYD'S *home.*

Clown (*enters*) Where he's been nobody knows, dirt on his fingers and grass in his toes.

Dorothy (*enters with tea towel*) What are you doing round here? Akroyd's in you know, he only has to look out of window, then you'll catch it.

Clown I already have.

Dorothy What?

Clown Caught it: Here: Who dwells in the country, wears a fur coat, lives on acres of land, and likes having his oats? No, it's not Lord Harewood, it's . . . a rabbit. (*Produces rabbit.*)

Dorothy Where did you get that?

Clown Back Shibden Hall.

Dorothy Put it away, you fool, or they'll have you.

Clown They nearly did . . . aye. I'd just got to me snare, back of the hall, when I heard gamekeeper coming down southside of wood wi' his dog.

Dorothy What, that bulldog.

Clown No, big daft thing wi' floppy ears. Anyroad, I flattened out right off. He goes past. I were pressed down that hard me knuckles had gone white. Suddenly me nose starts twitchin': Ah . . . ah . . . aah. Gamekeeper were deaf as a post, but dog heard, and comes trottin' over, like that. I'm still going ah . . . ah . . . and blow me if dog doesn't start lickin' me all over me face: slurp . . . slurp. Gamekeeper had got to top by then and starts whistlin' for his dog: whi . . . whi . . . whi . . . he goes, and starts back down towards me. What a mess. Here's dog going slurp . . . slurp . . . me . . . aah . . . aah . . . ah, and him going whi . . . whi . . . whi . . . Sounded worse than Huddersfield choral society on a bad night. Slurp. Ah. Whi. (*etc.*) 'Til I couldn't hold it any more . . . atchoo! Dog flew off wi' its tail stiff as a poker, gamekeeper spots me, come out say he, get lost says I, and upped and legged it over banktop. But not empty handed. A good fat un, eh?

Dorothy I don't care how fat it is, if they catch you stealing rabbits round 'ere – Wakefield jail and your feet won't touch the ground.

Clown Stealing! Stealing! Stealing is when you take things that belong to somebody else. I just took this.

Dorothy Shibden Hall belongs to the squire. You stole it.

Clown Take the rabbit from the field, and the grouse from the moor. Because the squire took the land that belongs to the poor. Eh? Have you got a use for it? Go on. I've plenty more snares set.

Dorothy If Mrs Akroyd sees.

Clown Go on . . . a feast for the family, take it home.

Dorothy Thanks. Now clear off sharpish before they see you.

Clown Ta-ta. Have a nice supper.

Lights up in the AKROYD's *home.*

Mrs Akroyd Dotty . . . Dotty . . . where are you?

Dorothy enters with rabbit behind back.

Dorothy Coming, maam. I was just seeing off a begger.

Mrs Akroyd Come along, the gentlemen have finished eating. It was very nice, Dotty. You can clear the dining-room now.

Dorothy Yes, maam.

Mrs Akroyd And don't let what's left of the beef disappear this time.

Dorothy No, maam.

Mrs Akroyd Ooh, this is nipping me a bit but how does it look?

Dorothy Lovely, Mrs Akroyd. Beautiful.

Mrs Akroyd Run along then, Dotty.

Enter AKROYD, MILLER *another employer, and* MAJOR BURNSIDE, *brandy and cigars in hands.*

Major A delightful meal, Mrs Akroyd, delightful.

Mrs Akroyd Oh, thank you, Major Burnside. Do sit down.

Miller You've done us proud, Mrs Akroyd. You're a lucky man, James. I don't know where you found her, but I wish I could do as well . . . eh, Major?

Major A lady who combines both beauty and an excellent table is a rare jewel indeed.

Miller Aye. I've been unlucky in love.

Mrs Akroyd You do surprise me, Mr Miller.

Miller Oh, there's been plenty sniffin' around. They stroke your hair wi' one hand and feel the size of your wallet wi' the other.

Mrs Akroyd Well, I'm sure you'll make the marriage you deserve one day, Mr Miller.

Miller Aye. Eh?

Enter DOROTHY.

Mrs Akroyd Yes?

Dorothy Excuse me, Mrs Akroyd, but there's . . . er . . . two people outside, wantin' to speak to the master.

Mr Akroyd Who are they?

Dorothy They're from mill . . . They say they've got a petition for you, sir.

Mr Akroyd All right, Dorothy, you'd better show them in.

Mrs Akroyd Oh, James!

Miller The damn cheek of it, comin' to your house 'ere on a Saturday evening. They've no respect.

Major What is it they want do you think, sir?

Miller What do they always want, brass.

Mr Akroyd We've recently been forced, Major, to reduce wages in the mills – a desperate measure and one which I personally very much regret.

Miller I bloody don't.

Mr Akroyd Trade is bad, Major.

Miller I don't know where it'll end. I wake up nights thinkin', have I done right to go in for mills. You give folk work and a fair wage and all they want is more, more.

Major But you were telling me earlier, Mr Akroyd, that you've expanded.

Mr Akroyd Yes, I have.

Major How can you?

Mr Akroyd I'll admit it's a risk. But I've got firm orders you see. Military contracts, and I can do 'em cheaper than most. I'm swimmin' against the tide, Major, but keepin' me head above water.

Major But your military contracts won't last for ever.

Mr Akroyd The whole thing's a gamble, when all's said and done, I've just backed me chances.

Miller You're a braver man than me, James. I've just battened down hatches wi' rest of manufacturers. Akroyd's a rebel, Major.

Major I admire your courage, sir.

Enter SARAH *and* ELSIE.

Mr Akroyd I think you'd better leave us, Annie, it may not be suitable for ladies' ears.

Exit MRS AKROYD, *passing the two women in all her finery.*

Mr Akroyd Now then, what is it?

Elsie We've been chosen to give you this, Mr Akroyd, on behalf of all the people at the mill.

Mr Akroyd All?

Sarah All that's life left in 'em, yes, Mr Akroyd.

Miller Don't be insolent, girl.

Mr Akroyd I suppose it's about adjustin' wage rates, is it?

Elsie It's about empty bellies and hungry children, Mr Akroyd.

Mr Akroyd I know that's how you're bound to see it . . . er?

Elsie Elsie Carter's my name, Mr Akroyd.

Mr Akroyd Elsie. But try to see it my way. If we can't agree a reduction, then all of us, the whole firm, me included will go to the wall. A small sacrifice now for a better future, that's the way to see it.

Elsie You can whitewash pump all you like, but the water still comes out the same – you're cuttin' our pay.

Mr Akroyd You either trust my judgement and good faith, or it'll mean hundreds more idle . . . livin' on parish.

Miller Oh, that'll not worry 'em, James. They'd be happy to get back on the scrounge again. Livin' off rates and taxes. See how we're fixed, Major, either way they're livin' off us.

Major Very true, sir . . . very true.

Elsie All I know is my bread, candles, everything I buy is taxed, and I see little benefit for it . . . and if I was livin' off taxes, I'd be in good company, Major.

Sarah We just want you to read it. People can't stand much more.

Mr Akroyd Yes, I'll read it carefully. I promise you. I'll see what I can do. (*Hands petition to* MILLER.) Now perhaps, if you're hungry, if you step into the kitchen, I'm sure they'll find you something to set you on your way.

Sarah No, thank you. There's better ways than that to put food in our bellies. We'll wait on your reply. Good night.

Exit ELSIE *and* SARAH.

Miller Here, listen here: 'We are reasonable and moderate in our aims, but if deprived of our due reward, needs must consider other means to have our rights.'

Major Do you think they mean a strike?

Mr Akroyd If they do, they'll ruin me. These next few months are make or break. Like I said, I've several large contracts offered me. If I can keep rolling I stand to make a fortune. If not, money, contracts, the lot, will go down drain, and I'll follow not long after.

Miller We're not all as well placed as you, James. You've no choice – if you give way, you'll put all rest of us in queer street. We agreed, everybody cut 'em a half penny an hour. You can't let us down, James.

Mr Akroyd You've heard news from yonside; half manufacturers in Stockport have gone bust. Ashton's in uproar. I agreed the cuts yes. But if that means riskin' ruin and riots in the street, then you've got to think again, Miller . . . Box clever, otherwise you'll play into the hands of every jumped-up Chartist and trouble-maker from here to Manchester.

Miller You're weakenin', James, we can handle 'em. The Major here's got troops ready and waiting in Leeds. If we show 'em a firm hand and a flash of steel, they'll come to their senses fast enough. They need showin' who's master round here.

Mr Akroyd Major?

Major I sympathise with your view, sir, a confrontation can be ugly. But in this situation I agree with Miller. Demonstrate a unity of purpose, disciplined ranks, and the rabble will disintegrate.

Miller Well said, Major. (*Screws up petition and hands it to* AKROYD.)

Mr Akroyd But can you rely on your men? Will they move against a strike?

Major They're hardened fighters, most have seen action in Ireland. No sir, none of them are local. They'll do the job thoroughly, I can assure you. They'll be glad of the exercise.

Mr Akroyd Well, gentlemen, let's hope it doesn't come to that. I only wish these things could be settled more amicably, if only people would listen to reason.

MILLER *and* MAJOR *exit.*

SONG OF THE SELF MADE MAN
Akroyd When I was a young lad

No more than a tot
I looked at all the other kids
I soon saw what was what.
The leader of my playmates
Was a five-year-old called Jim.
I made up my mind up there and then
That I would be like him.
He would go round all the toddlers
Taking all their toys away
And he wouldn't give them back to them
Until he'd made them pay.
Jimmy was my hero
That's how I began
To help myself to make myself
A self-made man.

Chorus.

O there's no use in helping one another
That never was of any use at all
For the strong will always get the biggest helping.
It can't be helped, the weak go to the wall,
So my advice is never help another.
And thank god the lord helps him who helps himself.
That's the way to make it in this wicked world
If you want the biggest helping help yourself.

When I'd finished schooling, I'd learned my ABC
That if you did your sums right, one and one should add to three.
I was taken as apprentice to a middleman called Pugh.
I saw him work, made up my mind, that I would be one too.
He would go round all the weavers, taking the homespun cloth
    they'd made
And sold it to the big man for twice what he had paid.
Old Pugh was my hero, he made me understand
How to help myself to make myself, a self-made man.

Chorus.

O there's no use in helping one another
That never was of any use at all
For the strong will always get the biggest helping.
It can't be helped, the weak go to the wall,
So my advice is never help another.
And thank god the lord helps him who helps himself.

That's the way to make it in this wicked world
If you want the biggest helping help yourself.

Now I've got my factory, I think I know the score
That if I keep on pushing, I'll have ten or twenty more.
I will be the big man, spreading overseas
And all the kids from everywhere, will want to be like me.
I'll be going round my empire, buying cheap and selling dear
It works just as well in Africa, as it does over here.
I will be the hero; my international plan
Help yourself to make yourself, a self-made man.

Chorus.

O there's no use in helping one another
That never was of any use at all
For the strong will always get the biggest helping.
It can't be helped, the weak go to the wall,
So my advice is never help another.
And thank god the lord helps him who helps himself.
That's the way to make it in this wicked world
If you want the biggest helping help yourself.

AKROYD *drops petition. Exits.*

Enter DOROTHY, *tidying away, finds petition.*

Dorothy Two days ago our Jenny were smashed into little bits by Akroyd's machines. I were listenin' outside the door. You know what Mrs Akroyd said, 'Vain foolish girl wearing a ribbon.' And he said, 'A great pity.' Look what he's done with this. Now hundreds of families goin' hungry and he'll probably say the same, 'A great pity.' Still, I'm not paid to think, I'm just paid to be Dotty.

Exit.

SCENE 12

Monday, sixteenth August. The St Monday Fair.

Enter CLOWN.

Clown Six days they said you should labour
And on Sunday get down on your knees.
So the people invented St Monday
And took a long weekend for their ease.
Long live St Monday.

Enter everyone available as the working people of Calderwike at the fair.

Where suitable, in character. The song should be accompanied with juggling, acrobatics, etc., if possible.

All sing Tuesday, Wednesday, Thursday, Friday working
Never have the chance to get things done,
Tuesday, Wednesday, Thursday, Friday working
Never have the chance to have some fun.
Saturday I'm much too tired I stay in bed
Factory hooter is still ringing in my head
Preacher has his holy day when he thanks his lord on high.
But I'll take Monday, St Monday, 'cos Monday is for life.

Clown The weavers are turning, spinners can dance
It could happen today at the fair, a fair chance.
Welcome to the great St Monday fair.

The entertainments of the fair begin. Anything ethnically suitable will do according to available skills. It should end, however, with the shuttle dance. We chose a clog dance, candle eating, a vendor of nuts and raisins in the audience, and the shuttle dance.

Clown And now, to start the celebrations let's have a clap for the clip clop of the Calderwike cloggers, accompanied by your very own John Greenwood on the fiddle and myself on the mouth organ. Put your feet together please for the Calderwike cloggers.

The Clog Dance.

Clown And now, friends, fellow feast makers of Calderwike, the next fantastic performance of these famous festivities is that fearless, frightening, death defying, and highly inflammable, Peter, the fire eater.

Enter PETER *with one or two lighted candles. We used burning almonds in the top of bananas to create the effect. He also needs a mug of water.*

Peter Stand back there please. Not too close, sir. You'll get your eyebrows singed. I have here firewater (*Shows mug.*) And flame. (*Shows candle.*) It's all right, madam, just duck, it'll go right over your head. Drums please . . . firewater . . . flame . . . keep your heads down in the front. (*Drum crescendo as he eats candle. Exit with applause.*)

Clown Peter the fire eater!? Terrifying. And last, my friends, to end our feast, let's hear you cheer for them that turns the world . . . the weavers' shuttle dance.

A traditional dance follows involving those available. It should be based on a sword dance but using shuttles in their place. JOHN *plays the fiddle.*

Clown Quiet now. Let's hear the fiddler speak.

John It suits me right well to play fiddle for a shuttle dance. Making merriment round our work you might say . . .

Clown It were grand.

John ... but, friends, the times have overtaken us it'd seem. The day has come for us to put down our shuttles. For the masters don't have no more use for the likes of us. And by Christ they've not taken the long road to let us know.

Clown Aye. Down with the bastards!

John Now don't get me wrong. I'm not against spinning-sheds and power looms. But it's a queer thing to me how with all these fine new machines, all turning out cloth enough for world I shouldn't wonder, that there's still folk suffering and starving to death. Aye, and the women and children slaving and dying in the mills from dawn to dusk, while other folk are thrown on scrapheap and worse. Brothers and sisters, will we stand by while the Akroyds of this land grow fatter and heavier on our backs?

Clown No! No! No!

John Shall we stay patient while our voices go unheeded and our demands go unmet?

Clown No! No!

John Or shall we say no? Shall we put down our shuttles? Shut up our looms?

The CLOWN *begins to collect the shuttles in a sack.*

John And take this sack to millworkers and shout: 'Shut down yer mills! Come out! We're with yer!' And joined together in a mighty throng, aye, with the Chartists of all Yorkshire and all Lancashire, with Bristol, London, Scotland, too, we'll proclaim the National Holiday is here! We'll call it the Sacred Month! A General Strike until we have the Charter. And then, at last, we'll get a parliament run by working people. And then, at last, we'll end the reign of poverty and degradation beset on all of us. Aye, and then we'll be sure those engines turn for us, our children and our grandchildren and cast off the yoke of Akroyd and his ilk. For the Charter! And Liberty!

Clown   The people speak out while they dance at the fair.
But there's more going on if you look here and there.
What the parson condemns and the masters all fear
The news that passes from ear to ear.
The Chartists of Lancashire are marching this way.
Tomorrow they'll be here. That's what they say.
Thousands and thousands the word goes around
Tomorrow's the day to turn this world upside down.

Three pairs have established themselves on stage: SARAH *and* DOROTHY, WILLIAM *and* AKROYD, JOHN *and* MARY. *All freeze in conversation. The* CLOWN *moves behind* JOHN *and* MARY. *They begin.*

John Tomorrow! I'll find Peter and the rest of them and tell them that it's on. They're ready, they know what to do.

Mary Tomorrow morning daybreak on Skircoats Moor. They'll come by the Turnpike Road through Mytholmroyd – that's the message.

John Have you seen Elsie? Are the millworkers coming out?

Mary There's still a lot waiting to see if Akroyd'll change his mind – waiting on that petition.

John Our Sarah among 'em. Fat chance.

Mary We must find Sarah and tell her what's happening.

John You do that. I've no patience with her. You tell her, Mary, if she cares about Jenny and what happened to her, to be there, on the Moor tomorrow. (*Freeze.*)

CLOWN *moves to* DOROTHY *and* SARAH. *They begin.*

Dorothy (*petition*) It's this: I found it last night after you and Elsie left.

Sarah The petition! Look at it. I'll bet he's not even read it. The bastard.

Dorothy A great pity.

Sarah What??

Dorothy That's what Mr Akroyd thinks – a great pity.

Sarah I'm going to take this down there tomorrow, and show it to the whole bloomin' mill. They'll tear him to pieces when they see this. Just wait 'til tomorrow. (*Freeze.*)

CLOWN *moves to* AKROYD *and* WILLIAM. *They begin.*

Akroyd You've heard the news from Oldham and Ashton have you?

William I heard some things . . . Chartists marching in' it?

Akroyd Worse. They're out to ruin all of us, lad. Forcing people into the streets. Breaking into mills, cutting off power, sabotage. We've got to protect our power, lad.

William Yes, sir. I know.

Akroyd Tomorrow once we've got steam up, don't let anyone in that engine room. Nobody. Understand?

William Yes, sir.

Akroyd Good. There could be a great future for you, William, if we weather this storm. Akroyds'll be biggest mill in Calder Valley, and I'll need a good man over it. I see you've already got an eye to the future. Who's the lucky girl.

William Oh, these. Yes, no. It all depends how things turn out.

Akroyd It always does, William. It always does. I'll see you tomorrow. (*Freeze.*)

Clown The fair has become a whispering hum,
What's happening tomorrow, what's to be done.

All break. CLOWN *sits backstage.*

Mary Sarah. Have you heard the news about tomorrow?

Sarah Yes. Have you heard the news. This!

Mary What is it?

Sarah The petition. Dorothy found it at Akroyd's. On the floor.

Mary Well, Sarah?

Sarah I'll show this down at the mill tomorrow and then they'll know what Akroyd really thinks.

Mary Good lass. Do you think they'll come out? Will they join us?

Sarah Most of them'll be out for blood when they see this. But there's a few so scared of losing their jobs . . .

Mary There's a way to make sure they all come out. Stop the engines and cut off the power.

Sarah How?

Mary There's a power house at the mill, yes? (SARAH *nods*.) In there there's a boiler. All you have to do is knock in the plug on that boiler and it'll run dry. Then, no more power . . . That's what they've been doing in Manchester and all the way across. And that's what we've got to do here.

Sarah But who could get in to do it?

Mary I could think of someone.

Sarah William! He'll help us.

Mary Do you really think he's on our side, Sarah?

Sarah Well, if he isn't after this . . .

Mary Find out, love. We must drive in that plug. The mills must come out. Tomorrow. (*Exit.*)

Clown Time to decide whose side you're on.
　　　　Make up your mind, the dance has begun.

William Sarah! I've been looking for you all over.

Sarah William!

William I've got something for you.

Sarah What?

William Close your eyes.

Sarah Don't be daft.

William Close your eyes. Right – now hold out your hand, go on . . . there. (*Gives her tidings.*)

Sarah (*laughs*) Tidings! Are you sure they're for me?! (*She opens them.*)

William Course I am.

Sarah I thought, after last Saturday, you'd have gone off me.

William No. It'd take more than that to get rid of me. I've been thinking . . . I might stay around here.

Sarah What about Manchester, and your great future?

William Prospects round here might not be as bad as I thought.

Sarah I'm glad you've changed your mind.

William I don't suppose you've changed your mind have you? About us.

Sarah I just don't know, William. We've not been walking out that long.

William Long enough.

Sarah I'm just not sure if I fancy getting wed.

William What you gonna do then, spend rest of your life in t' mill wi' that lot – daft girls and old women? Come on, Sarah. You can get away from your dad's interfering – we'll have our own place – everything – I'm earning a good wage.

Sarah What about me? What am I gonna do?

William How do you mean? We'll be married, Sarah. In't that enough?

Sarah I don't know ...

William Are you messing me about, Sarah? If you don't want me just say and we can pack it in now.

Sarah It's not that. I need to think a bit. I do love you, William, honest ... Here, have a brandysnap.

William Ta.

Sarah I've got something for you, William. It's the petition. Dorothy found it. We need your help, William.

William Who's we.

Sarah Everybody ... Chartists are planning big turn-outs tomorrow ... I told you they would.

William Oh, Sarah, you know what I think about that.

Sarah It's the only thing we can do. If I mean anything to you, William, I'm asking you please – help us. You will, won't you?

He kisses her.

William Course I will, love.

Sarah Promise ...

William All right, I promise, happy? But by next week it'll have all blown over, you see.

Sarah Oh no it won't, William. We've got to be ready – tomorrow ...

Voices Tomorrow. (*To be repeated all round audience in a mounting whisper.*)

Clown The fair has become a whispering hum.
What's happening tomorrow. What's to be done.

Voices They're coming
The Chartists
Skircoat Moor
At daybreak
National Strike
Be ready
Tomorrow
It's Time. It's Time. (*The whispering builds to a crescendo.*)
It's Time. It's Time. It's Time.

Music.

TAKING OUR TIME

John and Mary (*sing*)
The steady rhythm as the shuttle plays
I'm taking my time.
Working by hand in the traditional way

I'm taking my time.
The sun would shine on a lovely day
I'd walk in the countryside
And every Monday was a holiday.
I'd wave my work goodbye
I'd take off every Monday
I was taking my time
When the life I was living was mine.

The factory clock tick tocks the hours away
It's taking your time.
It never stops until you've earned your pay
It's taking your time.
The sun is out it's a lovely day
But they've got you locked inside
Five days a week you work your life away.
Your time is slipping by
Start by taking off Monday
Take your time back because
The life you are living is yours.

The day is coming, it's not far away
For taking our time.
We'll take the power and turn it our own way
We're taking our time.
The sun is out, today's the day
To take back all the time we've lost.
Not just Monday but every single day
We'll take it from the boss.
We'll make it this Monday
We're counting the hours
'Till the life we are living is ours.
Bridge music – 'Fair Song' theme.

SCENE 13

Tuesday, seventeenth August. Skircoat Moor, early morning.

Large Red Ladder set stage centre.

Enter CLOWN *with long red flag.*

Clown Today is the day. It's half past five and the sun's been up an hour.
Here we are at the top of Skircoat Moor. I can see shadows moving
about in the morning haze. Some have slept all night. Others like

tattered scarecrows stumble upwards. (*Climbs ladder.*) From Huddersfield and Halifax, Wakefield and Elland, up up up to the top. Me, I'm the look-out. From here you can see clear across the Calder Valley. The wail of factory whistles drifts up from near and far. How many will get knocked up and go to work as tho' it's just another day? How many will wake up and climb out of the dark mills to sit in the sunshine, waiting for the signal. The new day has started. A voice rises from the crowd to address a sea of faces.

Mary Word has come that the Lancashire lot have left Hebden Bridge. We will go down to meet them at Mytholmroyd. Then march to Halifax. And we're going to pull out every mill. Every work place. There could be trouble. Don't be provoked. They've had troops saddled and ready in Leeds for two weeks now. But I say we have been saddled by the masters and their lapdog parliament all our lives and it is time for us to throw them off. We will have the Charter, peaceably if we may, but forcibly if we must. We're almost ready to move now. Wait for the signal. Take your time. We'll get there.

Elsie Hold it out proper. (*A flag is held out reading 'LIBURTY' (sic)*). There, what do you think?

Peter Smashing. It'll go well at the front of the march. But it shouldn't be 'u' up there, Elsie.

Elsie Look, Peter, I spent all last night makin' this flag. And I'm the only one's going to carry it.

Annie No, no, he means it should be 'e' love.

Elsie I know he does. But it'll not be you and it'll not be 'e' – it'll be me what carries this flag.

Peter You spell this with an 'e', and not a 'u' . . .

Elsie Men! What's it say?

Annie Liberty.

Elsie What's it say?

Peter Liberty.

Elsie Right – that's what it says and that's what it means. And that should be good enough for anybody.

CLOWN *waves flag.*

Annie Look. The Signal. We've started. C'mon. (*They exit.*)

Clown Wave after wave across the hills the signal flies. The people flood down into the valley. But across the valley Major Burnside rises to address his troops. Row upon row of reds and blues. Sabres reflecting the same sunshine on the other side.

Enter MAJOR.

Major Right, lads. You know your orders. Don't fire unless fired on and use the flat of your sabre. And that does mean you, Johnson. Take it easy this time, lad, don't be carried away again. Now . . . there's rabble and there's some mean animals among them. Worse than the damn paddies

some of 'em. But we've handled it before. And if we have to go in, go in
hard, keep it tight. Let's make it as short and as sharp as we can. But
steady. And remember what I always say before this kind of exercise?
Right. We don't want another bloody Peterloo.

Clown The People are on the move. Every mill they pass the engines are
stopped. The plugs drawn. The crowd pours down the valley into
Halifax. In Halifax Major Burnside has ordered his troops to prevent
the crowd reaching Akroyd's Mill. Soldiers are stationed all over the
town. The people advance rushing and pressing along the narrow streets.
At every corner the soldiers block the way.

Enter MARY *and* SOLDIER *with rifle and bayonet.*

Soldier Now then, you stupid old bag. Clear off. Go on, get out of it. You've
no business here. (*He steps nearer.*) Move it or I'll shove this right up
yer. Get off out of it. Now. (*Steps closer.*) All right. You asked for it.
(*Swings back rifle. Stoops with bayonet inches from her throat.*) I'm
warning you.

Mary There's two ends to every gun, soldier, yours and mine. I know why
I'm on this end. But I don't know why the bloody hell you're standing
on t'other.

Soldier Move.

Mary Are you going to kill us all, son? There's kids here with empty bellies.
Fathers, mothers, family and friends. None of them your enemies. Are
you for keepin' us down, keepin' us starving? Go home, soldier, and tell
your wife and kids, tell your mother and your friends what you've been
doing today. Clear off. Go on. Get out of it. You've no business here.

Soldier (*gobsmacked, looks stage left*) You . . . you over there . . . go on!
Get off! Move it! (*Heads off away from* MARY.)

Clown Akroyd's Mill, the biggest in the Calder Valley, is surrounded. Akroyd
– the man who swims against the tide and hopes to ride out the storm.
For the people it is the beginning of a new day. For Akroyd it could be
the end.

The boiler room at Akroyd's. WILLIAM *is attending the boiler. Knock
outside.*

Sarah William. Let me in, William. It's me.

William What the bloody hell's tapping out there. (*Open.*) Sarah! You daft
bat! What the hell are you . . .

Sarah Hurry up, William. We've got to knock the plug. It's happened,
William. I told you it would, the whole of the Calder Valley!

William Calm down, Sarah, calm down.

Sarah Quickly, William, before they fetch the constables down. We've got to
do it.

William Sarah, best thing you can do is clear off home. I told you. It's mad-
ness, and I'm having nowt to do wi' it, nor should you!

Sarah But you swore you'd help us, you promised me, William.

William I am doing, if you could but see it, Sarah. This is not our fight. Your father and his Chartist lot are out to wreck Akroyd. All right, they've got nowt to lose – I have, Sarah – we have.

Sarah We! Who are we! There's bloody thousands of people out there, and they've got everything to lose, William. Everything.

William Not this way. It's useless. I love you, Sarah. I've worked my guts out to get where I am and I'm not jacking it in for that lot out there.

Akroyd (*enters*) What's going on here . . . (WILLIAM *turns to him*, SARAH *runs and picks up hammer by plug.*)

William I'm sorry, sir.

Akroyd What you doin'?

William Sarah, put that down.

Sarah We've come to knock in your boiler, Mr Akroyd.

Akroyd Don't talk nonsense, girl, put that down . . .

Sarah One step nearer and in it goes . . .

William For god's sake, Sarah!

Akroyd Now, listen to me. I don't know who's put you up to this, but it'll do you no good. So you close me down for a day, have your little holiday. I'll start work again tomorrow, but mark my words, you, nor any of that rabble out there'll ever work for me again.

Sarah Oh, it's no day's outing we're after. They're waiting out there and when they hear this boiler go off, it'll be the signal to let off your dam, Akroyd, every drop of water you've got.

Akroyd You're insane. (*He moves towards her.*)

Sarah I'm warning you.

Akroyd It'd take me six weeks before I could start up again . . . You'll bring us all down.

Sarah In six weeks we might have the Charter, Mr Akroyd. That's time enough for me.

Akroyd I can't give you the charter. I don't make the laws. Look, here's five pounds. Take it. Go out there and tell them. There's enough to buy bread and more for everyone of them. Take it. But for god's sake, let my dam stand.

Sarah Keep your money, Akroyd.

Akroyd I'll have you jailed for this.

William Sarah, think about us, you're destroying everything we've got, give it to me. (*Approaches her.*)

Sarah You bastard. (*Knocks plug. Sound. Light.*)

Clown It is the signal. The crowd burst into the yard. Tumbling up to the dam. They cheer as the slow gears grind the sluice gates open and Akroyd's precious water, his source of power trickles, spills and then begins to roar down the drain. Success. Suddenly a bugle and the clatter and ring of bridles and sabres. Panic. Heaving and pushing and screaming. As Major Burnsides goes in hard. Forging a way for the constables to wind back the sluice. Short sharp cuts and rifle butts set blood flowing. A volley fired in the air sprawls the crowd in a hundred different directions. The soldiers advance, bayonets first. The sluice gate grinds shut. Akroyd's precious water is saved. One trooper remains and looking the length of mill lane raises his musket and takes deliberate aim. He fires one single shot. (CLOWN *is shot*.)

Enter PREACHER, MAJOR *and* AKROYD.

Akroyd Congratulations, Major. Very cleanly executed.

Major Thank you, Mr Akroyd. They've done you no damage I trust.

Akroyd Just the boiler drained. We held the dam. We'll have power again tomorrow. Business as usual.

Preacher It's the Lord's work, Mr Akroyd. Discipline and restraint have triumphed over idleness and frivolity. The fool and the transgressor justly rewarded for their pains.

CLOWN *is dead on ladder. 'Clown Song' theme is played. He rises and comes down stage.*

Clown (*speaks*)

> Power
> Turns the world
> Brings you where you've come from
> Takes you where you're going.

> The Greenwoods of Calderwike and the Chartists of Yorkshire and Lancashire:
> Take their Time, their hopes and their dreams.
> Gone by.
> The clattering mills of Halifax and Bradford:
> The Dream of the Master and his Engineman.
> Here! Now.

> Power, their power,
> Turns the world.
> The Time is theirs, the twentieth century dream is here.
> From hard times to great expectations
> Now life is lived for a promise, as time passes by.

> The people are asleep.
> Are they dreaming the masters dream

Or will they once again wake
And take their own time.

Song, sung by CLOWN *and everyone.*

GREAT EXPECTATIONS

The roaring rattle clatter of the modern factory line
Twentieth-century dreamer.
Did you miss the bus, you're late, and have you got the time
Twentieth-century dreamer?
Working hard to earn your daily bread
(Worry hurry home each evening)
Listen to the silence in your head
(This breathless, senseless life you're leading).
The twentieth-century dream
The twentieth-century dream.

Great expectations
Hard times are still here.
Great expectations
While the time of your life disappears.

He's making multi millions from the modern factory line
Twentieth-century schemer.
An International Empire growing bigger all the time
Twentieth-century schemer.
His finger's on the switch that powers the world
(Wheeling dealing, he's here, he's there)
Leading us into tomorrow's world
(Making us live out his nightmare).
The twentieth-century dream
The twentieth-century dream

Great expectations
Hard times are still here.
Great expectations
While the time of your life disappears.
One life for the living, one time to go round
Twentieth-century dreamer.
Will you wake and take this world and turn it upside down
Twentieth-century dreamer?
They'll say that you're a clown, a fool to try
But take your time and live before you die.
Wake up from the dream
Wake up from the dream.

Great expectations
Your time is here.
Great expectations
Before the time of your life disappears.

END OF PLAY